'HER' INTUITION

SHE KNOWS BOOK 2

WITH HER INTUITION, SHE KNOWS.

CHRISTOPHER BLYTHE BARTRAM

DEDICATION

To
Donna C.,
She Knows

CONTENTS

ACKNOWLEDGMENTS

Madeline E. Buhr

Madeline E. Buhr / The Editor

Andrew Hess

Andrew graphics/Designer

SelfPubBookCovers.com/andrewgraphics

INTRODUCTION

Double talk—say one thing, but mean the complete opposite. Ever been told it's okay to go golfing with your friends when you flat out knew it was anything but okay? Ever been told to go away, but knew they meant stay? Many individuals have trouble understanding this, though it's even harder to spot when someone is doing it to you.

Don't you realize this is a prime example of them having power over you? '*She knows*' you will most likely decide to stay or not go golfing with your friends because the person doing the double talk is the one cooking your dinner, washing your clothes… They are the one with the… pussy.

Women know they hold the power. Strong women will know how to use this skill effectively with a vengeance. Defy them and run the risk of not getting any for a month, waking up with nothing to wear to work, or not having a packed lunch for work. She may go away for the weekend, leaving you with the kids, or you may come home to find your dinner still in the freezer.

Despite knowing full and well the "dangers" of dating, men so often waltz blindly into relationships, like walking straight into a Venus flytrap waiting to bite.

There's an old phrase, "if it's too good to be true, then it often is." The same idea applies to women. If she's too hot to be real, she probably is. You may see a woman, and yes, she may appear stunning with a really nice ass and gorgeous body with long silky hair. She just catches the eye of every red-blooded male out there, while all other women simply glare with a jealous rage.

However, you just know this woman means trouble. You know if you attempted to impress her, it would mean going up against every other man around. Then if you did manage to grab her attention, that would mean worrying about other men watching her the way you did at first sight. Can you trust your girl out of your sight? She knows your boss, so if you risk dating her and it goes bad, you know everything else will follow suit. You could even lose your job. You can see by her Facebook posts, she just loves attention and always responds to drama. attention and always responds to drama. It's such a sticky situation; she is a Venus flytrap.

Would you be able to resist her and walk away? You don't know? She knows!

Just leave me here of course

Look out the window lol

2 CHAPTER TWO

Mrs. Spoonman walked up to the entrance of Merv's Hot Bread Kitchen on Market Street. Before entering, she stopped to check the letter she received from her daughter, Lynn.

Four years ago, her daughter went to study in New York City in America. She had graduated from high school early back here in England. As Lynn's mother requested upon her departure to America, Lynn had been sending letters to her mother daily. She refused to email unless it was important. In her first letter, she wrote:

> *"It is more personal if I write to you than by sending email. You will know I took the time to personally sit down to write and put thought into what I want to write to you."*

Now, four years later, Mrs. Spoonman only occasionally gets a letter from her daughter, usually requesting her to send items from her old home that she could no longer get by being in America. The most recent list Mrs. Spoonman had received contained:

1. *Norfolk Knobs white*
2. *Bacon and Sausage Baps*
3. *Cornish Pasties*
4. *Cheese Straws*
4.2 *Large sausage rolls*
6. *Scones*

Mrs. Spoonman was about to walk into the store to purchase the items listed when she heard a voice calling out to her. It was Chris, one of the boys who'd had a crush on Lynn for as long as she could remember. He was also a friend of her son, John. John had been murdered by his own sister, Samantha. It had been discovered that Lynn's dad was John's father by another woman. Samantha found out John was going to divulge the information, so she killed him to keep the secret hidden; however, they found her to be in possession of a note revealing the truth.

"Hi, Mrs. Spoonman," Chris said happily as he approached her.

"Hello, Chris. How are you?" Mrs. Spoonman replied.

"Fine. You get another letter from Lynn? How she doing at college over there?" he inquired, sounding excited.

"I'm sorry, Chris," Mrs. Spoonman responded, knowing Chris would be disappointed by what she had to tell him. "She says she has a new boyfriend. She also got a part time job in this beauty store in New York. She is doing really well, just missing some of her favorite foods from back home," she explained, referring to Lynn's note.

"Oh. Well, thanks. Least she is happy then," Chris remarked, as his smile shifted to a disheartened frown.

"I'm sorry I couldn't give you better news," she said quietly, hoping this would finally give him the push to move on from his crush on Lynn. *Least it proves he is loyal,* she thought to herself.

Mrs. Spoonman made her way inside the store to retrieve the items Lynn requested be mailed to her in America. She waited in line and noticed Chris was still standing outside, appearing rather depressed as he stared down at an old photo of Lynn on his smartphone. Suddenly, Mrs. Spoonman had an idea.

Chris slowly started to walk away from the store to continue his journey to Woolworths. Just as made it to the other side of the street, his phone buzzed, signaling he had a Facebook notification. He pulled his phone out and sure enough, he had received a private Facebook message. A giant smile spread across his face as he read the message.

I know you miss me, I miss you too. Love Lynn.

~

"Who are you messaging?" Courtney asked.

"Oh, no one, just an old friend. Mum said he has been pining for me since I left," Lynn explained.

"Aww, poor puppy," Courtney chuckled. Lynn responded with a laugh. Lynn met Courtney when she was still new to New York. They first met in Topshop on 5th Avenue, where Courtney was accompanied by her boyfriend, Tom.

Tom had been abusive to Courtney, which infuriated Lynn. After being coached by Lola, Lynn arranged for Courtney and her to go out for a night on the town. However, when Lynn arrived, it was clear Tom had hurt her again. Lynn couldn't stand anymore, so she decided to confront Courtney's parents with evidence by holding Courtney in front of her mom. The evening turned violent when Tom became enraged by the situation. Courtney's dad ended up shooting and killing Tom to defend his family.

As a result, Courtney's dad was arrested, though the police were sympathetic to the circumstances, such that some officers admitted they would have done the same thing if they found out someone was harming their daughter. In turn, the law is the law. Courtney's father had just committed murder. If Courtney or her mother had fired the gun, it could have been considered self-defense. However, her father was not in immediate danger himself, so it could not have been self-defense. Therefore, he was sent to Rikers, New York City's main prison complex, to serve a four year sentence. Luckily, he was able to take a plea deal since this was his first offense. Everyone present for the trial was sympathetic, even the judge.

"Our hands are tied. You broke the law; you committed murder being the protector of your family, and sadly, it is my duty to punish you regardless, knowing full well I would have done the same," the judge explained.

Now, four years later, Lynn just turned eighteen. She had a four year head start over everyone else her age. At fourteen, she started college at New York State College, where she majored in Psychology and Application Science. For fun, she studied Criminal Justice as well. In her spare time, Lynn also received instruction from Lola, the manager and owner of Credo, a local beauty shop in New York.

Lola was the first person Lynn met who seemed to have a similar personality and similar interests. Lynn was smart and she knew the power she wielded. the skill to distract anyone she wanted. Lola had started to show her all the powers of a woman who knows, and Lynn, she knows.

"Do you miss your home?" Courtney asked, as she and Lynn continued walking.

"I am home," Lynn stated simply, as she discarded the disposable smart phone into a trashcan they passed.

~

Over at the police shooting academy, Sergeant Wilkinson was still in the shooting range. He had selected a modified grip for the handle. Following the lecture, he christened the gun, "Angel".

To successfully pass the course, he had to shoot consistently with no less than a 96% accuracy rating. If you got three bullseyes and two outer on one round, then two bullseyes and three outers on the next round, you fail.

"Hold it like this, runt. Bend your arm at the elbow more," Sarah commented. The instructor was watching.

"How come you don't keep your arm straight like in the movies?" Wilkinson questioned.

"Try it, find out for yourself," Sarah remarked, gesturing with an open palm for him to proceed.

Wilkinson raised the gun and positioned his one open eye to follow the gun sight. He aimed the gun slightly above the bullseye slightly higher to adjust for the arch and prepared to move his index finger to release the safety.

"OUCH!" Wilkinson screamed, as his weapon crashed to the ground.

Sarah had just made a karate chop movement at the elbow of his extended arm forcing Wilkinson to drop his gun.

"Now, try again with the arm bent," Sarah instructed.

Wilkinson, expecting the blow this time, waited for the pain to come. This time, though, all that happened with Sarah's strike was his arm moved down and right back up again, and the gun remained in his hand under full control.

"Okay, you've made your point," Wilkinson stated, rubbing his bruised arm.

"I hope so, runt. You lose your gun, you are out of the fight. Out of the fight, and you're dead. Also, it improves your accuracy this way. Use your other hand to cup the base of the handle," Sarah explained, demonstrating with her own weapon.

"Is there really that much of a difference?" Wilkinson asked.

"Show him, Sarah. Sergeant, the standard issue police gun like your one is rather easier to shoot, and the lady Sarah has—would you agree?— is a weapon with a kick to it, making it harder to aim."

Wilkinson agreed.

"Well, I have a Andrew Jackson to say Sarah's accuracy with a standard issue police weapon will be lower shooting with a straight arm than the accuracy with the Desert Eagle shot with a bent arm. Ten shots for each?" the instructor challenged.

Several other officers in the range all stopped when they heard the offering of a bet.

"I'll take that bet," one male officer shouted.

Wilkinson glanced toward the officer who accepted and turned back.

"Well, okay. If he is taking the bet, I will too. He looks like he knows what he is doing."

Sarah stepped up to her own shooting lane, picked up a random standard issue Glock 19 pistol. She held it with her right hand and raised it to eye level.

The target she selected was a black silhouette of a man. She fired five quick shots and the spray of bullets hit around the chest area. Maybe one got the heart, then one in the lung area, and two got the shoulders or collarbone. One shot to the far right was a miss. Wilkinson learned that one wild bullet meant one innocent victim dead and the reason for being sent home.

Sarah fired again after a brief pause, aiming for the head this time. Two went high, possibly giving him a haircut, and the others hit just around his head.

Sarah made sure to toggle the safety on again before disconnecting the bullet chamber. Then she placed the pistol and empty ammo clip back on the counter. Stepping up to a new target, she then turned to face her audience.

"Try not to cum in your pants boys." She smirked, as she reached into her cleavage and slowly pulled out her "Lady." It was a Desert Eagle made of finely polished silver with the female symbol engraved on the left side of the handle. The right side held the words, "Silly boys, guns are for girls," with an eight karat gold edge frame around the handle plates.

She turned to face the new target, switched off the safety and fired quickly. Bang, bang, bang, bang! The sound of the desert eagle reverberated throughout the gun range. Two bullet holes formed two eyes and the other three formed a little mouth over the center of the target. She fired another rapid four shots. One shot for each eye of the face, one for the nose, and one for the mouth.

She removed her ear protection from her left ear, and turned to see a rather dominating distinct shape forming in Wilkinson's pants. Sarah smiled to herself.

"You see enough, boys?" Sarah gloated, as she peered around the range at her audience.

"Wait, you only fired nine. You have one more shot to go." Wilkinson took Sarah's bait.

Without hesitation, she pointed and fired without even looking. This one last shot made all the men go limp, instantly losing that distinct shape in their pants, as there was a smoking new hole where the target's distinct shape would have been too.

"Get my point, runt? Now, pay up to the instructor and get back to learning. I'd like to actually crack some skulls."

She walked off, placing her *Lady* back into her bra holster, knowing full well all eyes were on her. Once again, she smiled to herself.

3 CHAPTER THREE

"So, you've come a long way since you first arrived here four years ago. Do you know what you want to do with yourself now?" Lola inquired, while restocking shelves with beauty products ready for the next customer.

Lynn started working at Credo over the summers between her years in college. At the moment, she was wiping down the counter.

"I'm tired of manual labor. Why I had friends for, so they do it for me," Lynn sighed.

"So, I see you are getting frustrated. Is it because you have to work for money to be able to live or is it because you are seeing you may have to settle with a mediocre life like the rest of us?" Lola replied.

"I'm frustrated because this is a huge waste of time. You are the owner of this store, so you have employees to do the work for you that you don't want to or have time to complete. I'm no henchman. I'm frustrated being in a lowly position; it's beneath me."–Lynn stood up, dropping the rag– "However, I've already initiated a plan, so I don't need to do this summer job anymore, and you can continue to train me and do more useful things."

"So, you want to lead? Well, you have to learn how to follow first," Lola commanded. She leaned over, picked up a broom handle and tossed it toward Lynn. "You need to sweep the floor. Despite how you may feel, these tasks are an important part of the training…"

The sound of the door opening interrupted their conversation. Two people entered Credo's, the New York City beauty store.

"Welcome, welcome! Name, please?" Lola rushed forward to greet the visitors.

The gentleman accompanying a woman presumed to be his wife announced, "The name is Hemlock. We have an appointment for your personal treatment." The wife looked around the shop as they entered, beholding all the bottles and instruments used for their crafts. She didn't notice her husband quietly dropped a small packet onto the ground. Before Lynn could blink, Lola snatched the broom back and swept the small packet out of the way and into her hand without the woman ever noticing.

"Ma'am, please have a seat here." Lynn turned and presented a chair for the woman to sit down. After the incident with the packet, Lynn was eager to ask Lola what was going on, but it would have to wait.

"Lynn, will you be okay starting the prep for Mrs. Hemlock while I take Mr. Hemlock to sort out his account in the back?"

"Sure. I can do that," Lynn replied, sounding distracted. She was all too interested in watching Lola take Mr. Hemlock into the next room, but Lola closed the door behind them.

Mrs. Hemlock sat down and Lynn started by putting on an apron. She started with a cleanse applying a face mask to Mrs. Hemlock's face. Then she spun the chair around and tilted it back for her to start wetting Mrs. Hemlock's hair.

Lola opened the door, and timidly asked, "Everything okay out here?"

"Yes, all is fine. You need help with anything?" Lynn responded.

"Nope!" Lola replied bluntly, making sure Lynn saw her lick her lips to get the hint across.

"So, you're Lola's young prodigy?" Mrs. Hemlock stated with a muffled tone, and lifted her face mask. "It isn't what it seems. Well, it is… He's getting the 'spit and shine polish' from Lola. He thinks I don't know, but he pays… I get a free session here, and it is quite fun watching him squirm about when the pressure gets put on him." Mrs. Hemlock reclined back again and replaced her face mask, as Lynn returned to the sink.

"I'm Sharon Hemlock," she introduced herself, extending her hand.

"I'm Lynn," Lynn responded, returning the handshake. "Don't you care that he is doing that?" Lynn asked, still feeling a bit unsettled by the whole situation. She didn't mind necessarily, but was just surprised.

"Dear, here is a free lesson. Men's eyes wander. It isn't their fault; you can't fight nature. And with people like yourself walking around, they will be watching your ass and tits. You know what I mean, I'm sure they glance at you and imagine fucking you from across the street."

"I've had the attention of both men and women, yes," Lynn responded.

"So, you are doubly cursed. This is one of the oldest games in the book from the days of kings and queens of Europe. The days where fifty year old men would marry fourteen year old girls as queens and announce engagements of their children to other royals' bastard children before they were even out of diapers," Sharon sighed. "Many of the queens did what they could to keep being the focus of their kings' attention because while you are his favorite, you get all the rewards that come with it. You have power; you can influence policy, or bend the ear of the man. Sooner or later, he would get bored with you, or while you are stuck for nine months carrying their child, or the many other ways men become bored mainly because, just like now, they see some hot new young thing like my husband just did with you.

"Then their interest is on the new slut. Then suddenly you lose that power, and this slut has the power, his "favor," and that slut becomes a threat and danger to you and your status. Don't get me wrong, I don't blame you for this either. You are young and innocent; it's how it always is, and it is that innocence that attracts the wolves. I have been in your position, where you are now, and you will be in my position soon enough."

Lynn now started the shampoo treatment after wetting Mrs. Hemlock's hair to untangle any knots, so as to begin washing her hair.

"So, what is the answer?" she asked.

"You control it, like you control everything else of your man's life. Men are dumb enough to think and believe we don't know what is going on. They telegraph it over their forehead when they're in love. You know it is going to happen, so you just make sure of who they are fucking. That is where Lola comes in. Of course, this normally means if you introduce your man to another woman that you prefer he fucks, instead of who he wants to fuck. Then of course you are saying to that person, 'I don't see you as a threat to me.' Some women take offense to that and try to exploit the situation to their favor, then you have to deal with them... Such a headache. However, Lola is one of us. You see, even though he is in there with her, thinking I don't know, in about a week's time, he will get a sealed envelope from someone black mailing him to give me $250,000 or they will tell me of his affair. The change is instantaneous and remarkable. He doesn't know who is watching or where, so he does everything to act nice around me and towards me. And again, I maintain my control, my power. I get rich.

"This lasts about six months before he thinks he escaped. Then he acts like a man again, and thinks he got away with it, and his attention wanders. Then I bring him here and start the process again; however, this will be the fourth time, so his luck is going to run out. I will just divorce him, then find a new man to start over again."

"What happens if you actually meet a man that is faithful and doesn't cheat? I mean, looking is one thing, but actually doing it is another," Lynn remarked, as she began to lather the conditioner.

"Honey, in the lifestyle you and I have come to expect and want, there is no gentleman like that around. Power corrupts absolutely. I have my fun too, with little side projects, as I call them," Sharon replied.

"I feel sorry for you," Lynn commented.

"Why is that?" Sharon asked.

"Because in your struggle to maintain power, that power is dependent on someone else, not on yourself. So, that power is an illusion. If you had no men, you'd have no money. No money, no power, no lifestyle, no control. You are the furthest thing from being independent. But that isn't the worse of it. You've never experienced love and that is why I feel sorry for you," Lynn explained.

Mrs. Hemlock sat up slightly and lifted her mask to look at Lynn, as Lynn noticed Lola had returned and was standing at the door where she'd taken Mr. Hemlock. Her arms were crossed and a proud smile spread across her face.

"She is ready for you now, Lola," Lynn reported.

Lynn walked across the studio floor, handed her stylist apron and tools to Lola, and briefly turned back toward Mrs. Hemlock.

"If you will excuse me, Mrs. Hemlock, I need to go be a threat to you," Lynn remarked, as she discretely licked her lips towards Lola and closed the door behind her.

4 CHAPTER FOUR

40.7931° N, 73.886° W. On a 413 acre island, extended by its inhabitants, lays the lie of New York City, an island resting on the East River. By physical location, this island is part of the Bronx district; however, it holds a Queens zip code, hence the lie. Queens, which includes Citi Field – home of the Mets, is the well-established 'nice' area of New York as compared to the Bronx. Anyone living in Queens would be happy and all too willing to allow the Bronx to have this piece of real estate. As such, residents of the Queens district will often tell you this island is part of the Bronx, which is technically a lie.

This island has been made famous by a variety of shows, sitcoms, and movies. It boasts itself as both a tourist attraction as well as a more permanent residence for some of society's less than respectable citizens. The facility is always open 24/7, and on 352 days per year, curious individuals may ride authorized buses to the island for a closer look at this dark sector of New York.

While it neighbors LaGuardia Airport runways, the only way on or off this island is via the connecting bridge or the underground train. Some call it "New York's Alcatraz," but of course, it's... Riker's Island.

Some brilliant architect decided to place a group of Little League baseball fields on the main land adjacent to the Riker's bridge entrance. If one of the residents managed to take a day trip, they would run smack dab into the middle of kids playing baseball.

The contrast couldn't be more drastic. As soon as you step off the bridge onto the main land, it feels like you've rejoined civilization. Even nature abandons you when you cross the bridge. New York could be enjoying a nice bright summer day with high temperatures, but once you set foot onto Riker's Island, all you feel is isolation as wind gusts from the river.

A white '98 Dodge Neon with blue and white New York City plates, obeying the signs, approached the guard booth at the start of the bridge and slowly came to a stop. The corrections officer stepped down and approached the side of the vehicle as the female driver presented her driver's license and entrance pass.

The corrections officer returned the items without saying a word, walked back to the booth, and pressed the button to raise the barrier as he returned to reading his book.

The car began moving again. Maintaining a constant 3 mph, the vehicle passed over the pressure plate that would normally weigh trucks and busses coming in and out. It records every vehicle's weight as you enter the facility. If you leave weighing more than, let's say, an extra 180+ lbs, you get to look forward to a vehicle search.

After slowly proceeding across the bridge, the speed limit was adjusted back to the city's usual limit of 25 mph. From ground level, it was difficult to tell, but from above, it was very clear which side of the prison held the "soft" criminals and those waiting for trial, compared to those in for more serious crimes, like murder.

As the Neon exited the bridge, the woman instantly felt eyes on her. She knew the security would be scrutinizing every detail of her arrival. She pulled up to the security check point at the Perry Control Center. Again, she presented her entrance pass and ID. After an officer ran a mirror underneath the car, it passed through a stationary x-ray machine, and was directed to proceed. This was Hazen Street. To the left, the buildings looked as miserable, dirty, and unwelcoming as you could get. However, the buildings on the right side were painted white and appeared clean and tidy. While they still had bars on the windows, as it was still jail, the right buildings instantly gave off an overwhelming feeling that if you were sent here, you might actually survive prison life. In contrast, on the dark left side, you wondered if the flies and spiders were even afraid to go. There was no sign of wildlife, not even birds.

The Dodge followed along until reaching a junction in the road, and proceeded to turn left. It followed the road around to the corrections center entryway and found a spot to park.

The woman cut the engine, looked in the visor mirror, and licked her lips. She instantly grabbed some lip balm from her purse and applied it while looking in the mirror. She located her compact next, but opened it to become disappointed.

"Dammit, the powder is out," she remarked. She quickly grabbed her lipstick and applied it to her lips. Sighing, she decided to get out her blood sugar test kit. She added a fresh lancet to the punch and pricked her index finger. She massaged her finger to produce more blood and rubbed it in a circular motion on her cheeks to add a bit of color in place of blush.

Once everything had been returned to her purse, she opened a couple of buttons at the top of her shirt, and pushed her breasts up, so plenty of cleavage was visible. She blew herself a kiss in the mirror. Sighing, she exited the vehicle and stood there facing the big wired gates.

She had decided to wear a thigh length dress without any panties. As the breeze blew up her dress between her legs, she began to regret that decision. She felt cold despite the bright sun shining down with glorious heat. The cold mist and overall dampness from the river was overpowering.

She waited and waited. Periodically checking her cell phone, 10:30am and 11:00am passed. 11:30am passed, then midday came and went. She was sitting in the car's driver's seat with the door open when she finally heard the blaring buzz, which signified the gate was opening.

She stood up and saw him. A man carrying a package wrapped with rope walked up to the gate, escorted by two guards. He shook their hands before leaving. The man strolled through the gate, and once he

saw the bombshell waiting for him, nothing could stop him from running towards his wife and enveloping her in his arms.

He dropped the package and gave her the tightest hug imaginable. She kissed him for the longest time, as if they were sixteen all over again. He felt his "welcome home" gift that was waiting for him. As he squeezed her butt cheeks, he realized she had gone commando. She winked at him.

"I've missed you, my hero," she cooed. "Come, I've cleaned out the back seat. Let's find a quiet place, then we can head home. Courtney is waiting at home for you, but I want you all to myself first. Four years is a long time!" Courtney's mom exclaimed to her husband, as he went around the vehicle to the passenger side.

The white Dodge Neon started to pull away, heading back towards the bridge.

A dark grey Ford SUV with tinted windows started its engine and followed.

4.2 CHAPTER FOUR POINT TWO

"Not that I do not applaud you for your display of girl balls," Lola started. "And it was wonderful to watch from an outsider's perspective. However, when you responded to Mrs. Hemlock, were you doing your best to insult or harm her?"

"Yes, I wanted her to know that I was a threat to her and all women like that. They undo all the work that we try to do, all too happy to lay on their backs underneath men, while we been struggling to be the ones on top," Lynn replied.

"Well, don't you see the problem with that? Doing your best to harm her, I mean," Lola replied. Lynn shook her head in response.

"Well, I want you to think about a couple of things. When Mr. Hemlock came in and I grabbed the broom to sweep up the packet? I want you to remember your reaction, then ask yourself why you felt that way.

Second, what allowed you to get away with what you did to Mrs. Hemlock and what does the two have in common with each other?" Lola had dimmed the lights to the shop down to a very low lit glow.

Lynn pushed all the islands from the shop together to form a makeshift table.

"How is your friend, Courtney?" Lola asked as she laid down a hot pink poker tabletop on top of the islands.

"She is fine. Her dad got let out the other day," Lynn replied.
Lola unlocked the door, but didn't open it.

"Well, I invited an old friend of yours to help with the training tonight. Still thinking about those things?" Lola inquired.

Lynn didn't get to respond, as a woman approached the door and entered Credo's.

"Hmm, I'm ready for our 'act-like-guys' night," the woman announced, as she belched and held up an open can of Budweiser in her right hand. She also had a bag of goodies hanging from that arm, while she held a sealed 24-pack of Budweiser in the left hand with another 24-pack wedged under her left arm.

Lynn had not seen this woman in a good long while, as she no longer needed her service. It was Ann. Born and bred of the Bronx district of New York City, she had been Lynn's guide when she first arrived in the city.

Ann was wearing tight fit MOTO Floral Embroidered Mom Jeans with a poplin shirt under a black leather jacket. She sported MONIQUE rimless retro sunglasses as well.

Lynn wore MOTO White Lace Up Jamie Jeans with just a simple black tulle t-shirt on. Suddenly, she felt underdressed compared to Ann. She waited for Ann to put everything down before walking over to give her a welcome hug.

"Ladies, entry fees, hang them on your chairs," Lola ordered.

Ann immediately reached inside her shirt, removed the straps of her bra, pulled her bra from beneath her shirt, and hung it on the corner of her chair.

Lola undid the buttons to her Tie Dye Shacket and removed her silk bralette, leaving the shacket open. She hung it on her chair the same way as Ann.

"I guess you've done this before, Ann?" Lynn asked, as she followed suit after a brief pause.

"Yep, this isn't my first rodeo," Ann chuckled.

"We can't exactly be girls *acting like guys* if we are dressed like girls, and well, this just ensures the first part," Lola explained, as she sat down.

"Okay, as normal, your bras start you off with the initial buy in of $200. I'll explain for Lynn, as this is your first time. The Sally Hanson nail polishes are $10, Essie's are $5, Sinful Colors are $1. The winner will get $400 of stylist quality beauty products. The game is Texas Hold'em. You said, Lynn, you know the rules of poker?" Lola paused, allowing Lynn to respond with a nod.

"So, you know how to play, good, so now starts your training. Poker... Some will say it is about skill or luck; however, you can manipulate both if you know how to play people. Did you notice how Ann is wearing sunglasses at night?" Lola gestured toward Ann, as both Lola and Lynn looked towards her.

"So, what does that tell you?" Lola questioned.

"That she is trying to hide she is drunk?" Lynn guessed.

"Try again. Think of what it would have to do with the game," Lola prodded. Lynn tried to think what eyes would have to do with the game and what good hiding would do.

"Well, clearly if she is hiding them, the purpose of hiding is to stop other people seeing them. Their eye movement betrays when they have a good hand?" Lynn offered as an answer.

"Yes... although, there is more to it than that. Not revealing when you have a good hand or a bad hand, being able to keep a straight face. However, Ann walked in here wearing them, drawing focus to them. So although what you said is normally correct, in this case, it is flipped because she is wanting you to believe her eyes betray her–her 'poker face.' She will be able to play with your mind, attempt to make you think she has a bad hand for example, when in fact she doesn't. People are often afraid to admit weakness, not put it on display, so the fact Ann did means it was by design. Be watchful of that in future," Lola instructed.

"Antes in, girls." Each of the women placed a Sally Hanson nail polish in the center. Lola dealt two cards to all of them, then discarded two cards.

Lynn picked up her two cards and found she had an 8H and 6S. Ann was sitting to Lola's left, so she started the round.

"I bet 20," she remarked, pushing two more Sally Hanson's into the center of the table.

Lynn picked up her cards again to take another look at them.

"I call," she stated, matching Ann's bet.

"Call," Lola spouted instantly. She proceeded to deal the flop and placed three cards down on the table–AH, KS, 8C.

"I bet 50." Ann pushed an Essie in without even looking. Lynn again picked up her cards.

"Just fold already," Lola and Ann commented in unison. "You've already telegraphed you have nothing," Ann remarked.

"How?" Lynn asked.

"Because you keep looking at your cards. If you had anything, you wouldn't need to keep reminding yourself, and if you wanted us to believe you had something when you actually had nothing, you still don't look at your cards," Ann replied. Lola nodded her approval.

"Fold," Lynn stated simply.

"Call," Lola announced, instantly matching Ann's bet. Ann checked, Lola checked, and then proceeded to deal the turn card–JS. Now, all the cards on the table were AH, KS, 8C, and JS.
"Bet," Ann declared without hesitation, as she pushed another Essie bottle to the center of the table. She returned her sunglasses to her face, and proceeded to open another beer.

Lola paused and watched every movement Ann made before stating, "Fold."

Ann scooped up the pot, leaving a Sally Hanson for her next ante.

The cards were scooped up and placed on the bottom of the deck. Each woman was dealt two cards again.

"Fold," Lynn remarked, right after seeing her hand–7, 2. "WHP." Worst hand possible.

"Never tell what your hand was before the hand is over. We now know two cards that are out of the game," Lola reprimanded.

"Heads-up," Ann said, looking at her cards.

"Bet," Lola stated.

"Fold," Ann responded instantly.

"How come you let her collect the pot?" Lynn questioned.

"Because she wouldn't have bet unless she had a decent hand, unless she was lying, but I didn't have a hand worth challenging with."

Next round, Ann bet first, and Lola called. Ann bet again and Lola folded.

"What the hell?! You didn't even draw cards that time!" Lynn exclaimed.

"She re-betted, so I knew she had a high-end pair." Lola nodded to Ann, signaling her to flip her cards over, which revealed a JS and JC. Lola only had a KH and 10H.

"How do you know the cards that would have come up wouldn't have helped you?" Lynn wondered.

"I don't, and you're right I could have had 5 cards come up that made me win and Ann lose; however, you have to judge the risk. It would mean risking a lot for not that much of a gain and the chance of me getting something while she already has a pair outweighs me winning, so I folded."

Next round, Lynn finally got a decent hand, two Q's, and she smiled.

"Fold," Ann and Lola chimed in unison.

"But!" Lynn immediately cried out, as a shocked and sad expression came over her face.

"You told us you had a good hand," Lola explained.

"How?" Lynn inquired.

"Would you have smiled if you didn't?" Ann responded, finishing Lola's lesson.

"You still thinking about those things I told you to think about. Do you have an answer yet or do you need to see more?" Lola watched Lynn expectantly.

"Yes, when you took the broom, you surprised me. I wasn't expecting it. I underestimated you because you never demonstrated moves or skills like that.

"I got away with talking to Sharon because it was unexpected, and quickly, she underestimated me," Lynn finished answering. She quietly wondered why school never taught her lessons like this. She thought back to the time in Robert Kett Middle School where her friend Chris would play poker for lunch money on breaks back in England.

"When you did what you did, you basically smiled at her just like you did at your hand just now." Lola reached over to grasp Lynn's hand. "I'm not saying not to do your best or try hard, I'm saying just don't show it to people so openly. Sharon will always expect that from you now, what you displayed to her. She will never underestimate you again, which can cost you.

"Always do your best, but stop short of doing your utmost best in front of people. Allow people to think that what you do is your 'best,' so when it comes time to strike, they will always underestimate you and you will have power over them. Control the situation instead of the situation controlling you... Do you understand?" Lola looked directly at Lynn to ensure she was getting across the seriousness of the matter to her.

"Even if that means playing down your intelligence, appearing to be slower than you really are or not as strong, never reveal your full strength."

"Or simply put, get a poker face and use it in everyday life," Ann added. "You already know how to distract," she hinted, as she opened her shirt to reveal her breasts. This definitely got the point across, as Lynn's attention focused on her Ann's breasts just for the split second her shirt was open.

"I think I understand," Lynn replied.

Lola slowly let go of Lynn's hand. The women carried on playing poker for the night; Lynn was soon out after chasing a straight.

It came down to Lola and Ann facing off with each other. Round after round, one bet while the other folded instantly. On occasion, the other person would call the bet when they believed they might have something slightly better. If the original person didn't bet again, they would fold.

Twice, Lola and Ann split the pot with identical pairs of J's. Finally, Ann was dealt the bullet A, A.

"All in!" Ann declared, as she pushed her short stack into the center. This would normally make Lola fold; clearly this indicated Ann held a high pair. However, this time, Lola had a high pair as well—cowboys: K, K. Lynn, who became the dealer after going out, dealt the flop.

8S, 8D, KD. Lola's face betrayed her, as she allowed a beaming smile to appear. The turn revealed JH.

"Oh, come on!" Ann shouted, no longer able to stand the tension. The river card was flipped and Ann gave a rampant cheer as the third A in the deck was facing up at them under the dim lights.

Ann reached over, rounded up all the Essies, Sinful Colors, and Sally Hansen bottles to pull them toward her.

Lola smiled with humility and awarded Ann her prize of beauty products, in addition to allowing her to keep all of the nail polish bottles.

"Poker, like chess, teaches you about life; it teaches you to read people. You need to find an online poker site, I don't care which one, and practice until you can use every advantage you have. Because, as you witnessed, the skill is being able to read the body language of people. If you don't master this skill, you at least need to be aware of those that can master it, who will take advantage and twist the signs to trick you. Else you won't get very far in life without someone playing you, especially if you want to stay ahead in that 'game' of yours," Lola explained, summing up her lesson for Lynn, as she handed Lynn her car keys.

"Now, go over to Courtney's. You need to keep up with the pretense you built up thus far with her. After the final step, she will be your actual friend that would be willing to do anything for you. A useful tool to have."

Taking the keys and giving Ann a hug goodbye, Lynn obeyed her instructions and drove her ruby-red-colored car over to Courtney's house, which she had done many times before. After the 50 minute drive, she turned onto Courtney's road. Just as she was about to slow down outside Courtney's house, she quickly restored her speed to 25mph and drove past.

A dark grey Ford SUV with dark tinted windows sat to her right side as she drove by Courtney's house. Lynn waited until she turned off the street and got around the block before activating the Bluetooth call feature in her car, which was connected to her cell phone, and dialing Lola's number.

"Lola, we have a situation."

978-0692579237 (C B Bartram Books)

6 CHAPTER SIX

Over on Mill Lane just outside Lynn's former hometown, a large house stood proud at the end of a row of council houses. However, there were obvious signs of child play about the house, evidence of children living here. Bikes, balls, dolls, and other toys scattered the lawn.

Chris arrived on his bicycle and hopped off as he was slowing down. There were loud noises coming from the house he was heading toward, so being cautious, he decided to take it slow. He grabbed his cell phone and opened his contacts to start a text.

"Hey, I'm outside," he wrote, thinking it would be best to wait until later to ask if everything was okay. He didn't want to embarrass whom he came to see.

Chris heard a door bang open, followed by the shrills of a girl he knew to be Tru. Tru was a 15 year old girl of medium build and average height with blonde hair hanging down below her ears. She had a couple of curly bangs in front, which had always made Chris wonder how bored she must be to spend time to curl just two strands of hair. *I'll never understand women,* Chris thought.

"Hi," Chris announced, trying hard not to appear creepy again and ignoring the fact he appeared to have walked into an argument. Tru made her way over to the shed and retrieved her bike. As she pushed it past him, she just glanced over, nodded, and hurried away without speaking. With how red her cheeks were, she was clearly mad.

"You going to stand there all night?" came the sound of a female voice. Chris had been distracted, watching Tru ride away. He failed to notice the person he came to visit had finally appeared.

"Sorry," Chris replied. "I was saying hi to Tru," he explained with a guilty tone.

"Hmm, sure… and looking at her arse as she went by too, right?" she teased. "Come on up to my room." She turned and waved her hand, indicating her desire for Chris to follow her into the house.

"No, I wouldn't! She's your sister and too young," Chris objected.

"Oh, sure!" the girl laughed. As they crossed the threshold into the house, there was more shouting coming from the living room, much louder this time. The girl ran inside, grabbed her coat, and immediately turned around, pushing Chris back to make him turn around.

"Where is Fia?" Chris asked, politely ignoring the awkward situation.

"Out. She sleeping over at one of her school friends'," she answered. "You can leave your bike here." She pointed behind the shed.

It was clear something was going on, something that would send people running. However, out of respect, Chris didn't bring it up. He knew that when she wanted to talk, she would.

This was Raven, oldest of three daughters at age 17. Chris originally met her in high school; she was a year behind Chris. He was a computer prefect, so much of their time together was spent in the computer room. While he provided support to people and maintained the network of twenty two Macintosh II computers running System 2, she would spend hours upon hours, between both lunch and after school, wasting time in the computer room until she was able to become a computer prefect too.

After Chris left school, he did not see anything of her for a long time. After receiving the text message from Lynn on the way home, Chris had bumped into Raven. This was the first time they had seen each other in over a year.

After some convincing, she submitted to Chris' charms and agreed to become his girlfriend. Since then, this was only the fourth time he had come to call on Raven.

Raven was an inch and a half shorter than Chris with long straight brown hair, small round glasses, and braces.

She was very much a tomboy, but she had her girlish things too. She dreamed of driving a Porsche 911 one day, as did Chris. That was one of the few things they both shared.

"You mind if we just head up to the park up the road and just hang out?" Raven asked timidly.

"Sure, you okay?" Chris finally asked.

"Yea, I'm out of minutes on my phone," she replied.

Taking her cue, Chris suggested, "We can head to town on my bike and get you some minutes…"

"Nah, it's fine. He brought us all minutes, just didn't have the chance to put it on yet," she said, avoiding all eye contact.

Chris reached out and grabbed her hand to hold as they walked. Raven gripped his hand tightly in return.

A random car drove by, filling the silence. They were in the countryside of Norfolk, England four miles out of town. It could be anywhere from two hours to eight hours before a car might come up this road.

It was just a short eight minute walk before they came across the rectangle of open green space. It wasn't the Reck by any stretch of the world, not much of a park either; however, it was a very picturesque scene that looked more suited for an Agatha Christie Murder series episode.

It had a see-saw and little merry-go-round, along with a three seat swing set. They both made use of the swings as they admired the scene around them and occasionally stared into space.

They sat there in silence for a full fifteen minutes. Chris, still holding her hand, was just waiting for Raven to pick the time she wanted to speak.

"I'm moving to Watford and living with my dad," Raven eventually sighed.

"What?! Why?!" Chris burst out, sounding surprised. Watford was a good fifteen to twenty minute car ride from where he lived. It was too far to ride there on his bike, unlike her current home.

"How we going to be able to watch The Tribe with you in Watford?" Chris pondered. The Tribe was a TV show based in New Zealand about a tribe of children who had to survive on their own after a deadly virus killed all the adults. The show only aired once a week on channel four. Raven had introduced Chris to the show, and since then, they both found it to be their favorite show.

Raven chuckled. "Well, I don't exactly know how I will be able to survive Saturdays without watching our weekly dose of The Tribe," she replied sarcastically. "But I don't have a choice. Now, my father has his own place and settled. He came over today to pick us up like he normally does, so we can spend the weekend over at his; however, he demanded to my mom that either one of us come live with him or all three of us move in with him.

"So, I am moving in with him. It's better this way," Raven mused.

"How is it better this way? He can't just take you like that. Why is your mom letting him walk over her?" Chris questioned, sounding exasperated.

"She doesn't work, is living on welfare, barely moves, and smokes forty cigarettes a day, and does nothing but watches TV. I don't think it would take Child Services too long. Besides, the house is too small; I'm sharing my bedroom with my mom. Besides, you've seen him. He stabbed someone through the hand with a compass, pinning their hand to the table.

"He broke into a chemist's to steal condoms on a dare."–Raven turned to look at Chris–"If I didn't pick to go live with him, he would have taken all of us. I have to protect them from him. He would have taken me today, but my 'room isn't ready' yet."

"What do you mean 'protect them'? What is he going to do? Why not go to the authorities?" Chris questioned.

"Can't. Don't worry about it,"–she quickly jumped up, avoiding looking directly at Chris–"Let's go back, he should have left by now."

Chris knew not to try and pry for more of an explanation. She had said all she would. If he kept pushing her to talk, that would just force her to clam up even more.

"So, how long do we have? So I know the time frame. We have to have as much fun as we can," he remarked.

"Dad said he wants me to come help him finish decorating the room next weekend. He is *letting* Mum have us for this weekend," she replied.

"I'm sorry," Chris stated simply.

"For what?" Raven asked. This kind of put Chris on the spot.

"For being helpless... For not being able to help you," Chris responded slowly.

"Just let it be. I don't want you to help. It has to be this way." They had just gotten back home and made their way up to Raven's room by going up the stairs of the small two story house, ignoring her mom on the way, who was already watching the TV as if nothing had happened.

Instantly, you could see how cramped the house actually was. Directly at the top of the stairs, there was one bedroom to the left, which Tru and Fia shared. The one and only bathroom in the house was to the right.

Directly opposite the stairs was the master bedroom. As soon as you entered the room, there was a twin size bed to the left with just enough space to walk between it and the main bed, which was her mom's.

On the wall and the ceiling were pictures of boys and bands she liked. Her tape deck sat atop the dresser crammed between the bed and the wall.

Raven and Chris shared the passion of music. They would often listen to her favorites or to the radio while they laid together and held each other.

"You know what I told you before about my ex?" Raven asked Chris, as they sat on her bed together.

"Which ex?" Chris asked, poking fun at her.

"The one before my soon to be ex-boyfriend if he isn't careful," she retorted, as she playfully jabbed Chris' arm.

"What about him? No offense, I don't exactly like to remember people you were with before," Chris answered flatly.

"All boys want is sex. My last boyfriend didn't want to wait. So, the next time I saw him, I told him we would do it. I sat down opposite him, he took off all his clothes, and I got up and left," she finished, with a proud smile on her face. "However, when we, you and I, first started dating, I asked you to wait a year. I was still 15, underage by one year. It was hard to wait for a year, I know."

"Wasn't that hard really," Chris interrupted.

"Oh, so I'm ugly to you?" Raven exclaimed, pouncing on the hole Chris just dug for himself.

"Because I love you. Sure, there was times I wanted to do it and there were times I couldn't wait anymore, it seemed. But we pushed each other through." Chris placed his hand on her knee.

"Well…" She tried to ignore the 'I love you' part, except her face blushing revealed her true emotions. "You did wait for me. It means a lot. It shows you were serious, and that proved that you do love me and not in it for just the sex."

"The best things are worth waiting for. We are each other's first love. First real love, that is. We will never forget each other," Chris mused.

Raven leaned forward and kissed Chris passionately, forcing him down onto the bed for her to lay on top of him. Suddenly, she stopped kissing him to lift herself up on her elbows.

"What you thinking about?" she asked him.

"Your boobs," he replied honestly, as her cleavage was directly in his line of sight. "They look cramped."

"You better set them free then," Raven replied flirtatiously. She leaned back down to continue kissing him. Chris began to lift up the cups of her bra when she quickly slapped his hands down and shot back upright on the bed, as Tru burst into the room.

"Dinner!" Tru announced with a smirk on her face, seeing the two of them. Then she immediately left to go back downstairs.

"You coming?" Raven said to Chris as she jumped up from the bed.

"I'll be down in a bit. Need the bathroom first," Chris replied.

"The beauty of girl boners," Raven laughed, as she began to make her way down the stairs.

Left alone, Chris stood up and took the two steps needed to get into the bathroom.

He pulled out his phone and unlocked the lock screen. It opened to where he was last viewing, the Facebook message from Lynn.

I know you miss me, I miss you too. Love, Lynn

It was four years ago now when Chris almost landed in jail because of one of Lynn's schemes. She left the country, but Andrew, Luke, and himself, basically her hench-boys, still carried out her plan, which resulted in Vicky's death.

If it wasn't for his friends, Lorraine and Louise, he would be behind bars right now. He wondered though… *what if Lynn could come up with a plan to help now?*

Raven was being forced into a situation she did not want to be in, against her will. She believes she is protecting her sisters, but he didn't fully understand from what exactly. Chris did know her dad was not exactly a pleasant guy.

He knew it would be going against what Raven had said to him. *She may not even reply,* he thought. *What is the worst she can say? No?*

"Yes, the account is still active. She didn't delete the Facebook account," he quietly said to himself.

He flipped to the messenger section, and paused, trying to decide what to actually write.

"YOU COMING?!" Raven suddenly shouted up from downstairs.

"YEA, JUST A MOMENT," Chris hollered back.

Quickly, he typed his message. *Hey, Lynn, missing your skill and talent. My friend, she is in trouble. She needs your help.*

He hit send, sighing. As he left the bathroom to go have dinner with his girlfriend, he felt like he had just signed up to work with the devil.

7 CHAPTER SEVEN

"Dad!" a high pitch scream rang out, as Courtney bolted to the man who just came through the front door. Knocking the wind out of him, Courtney flung her arms around her father in a massive hug.

"Give him some air to breathe, Sis. I doubt he wants to be suffocated, having just got home," her brother, Michael, said. He came walking up the hallway with a big smile.

"No, no, it's okay. You suffocate away. It's the best feeling ever. There is room here for you too…" he said, coaxing his son toward him. Michael held off, waiting for Courtney to step aside. Once she moved, Michael extended his hand to shake his dad's hand. As soon as their hands clasped, their father pulled Michael in for an embrace.

"You are not too old to be hugged by your old man."

Courtney's mom slipped into her husband's arms after Michael had been released. They made their way into the main room, leaving Courtney to close the front door. Just as she was closing the door, she noticed a strange car pull up across the road, but Courtney didn't give it a second thought. She was too focused on the fact that the person who sacrificed himself for her had just returned home from spending time in prison.

"Courtney, get in here!" her dad hollered. "You need to tell me everything I've missed."

She ran into the living room, entering into a scene one would expect from a TV sitcom, and she was going to enjoy the moment.

"What happened to your friend from that night? Are you still talking to her?" Courtney's father questioned.

"Yes, Dad. We kind have become good friends. We go to the same college. She helped me carry on with my help that I received after my counseling. I know what Tom was doing was controlling me and manipulating me, and it was not right. I deserved better. That Tom never loved me, well, perhaps a little, but it turned into something worse."–she paused for a moment–"It really helped having a friend, someone not family, to talk to."

"Good. If possible, can you invite her over? I wanted to thank her. Although I am sure she didn't plan any of that to happen, I am glad she told us what was really going on with you and him.

"Invite her to dinner tomorrow, so we can thank her properly. I don't regret what I did for one moment."

"Sssh now…" Courtney's mom tried to interrupt, not wanting to relive that horrific night in their history.

"No, dear, this is important. Indirectly, she helped. What is her name?" he asked, as he turned toward Courtney.

"Lynn," she replied simply.

"So, it is settled. Please invite her to dinner tomorrow," her father declared.

Michael entered the room with two cans of Coor's Lite in his hands. He walked over to hand his dad a beer.

"Ah, thanks for getting your mom and me a beer, but I don't think she is much of a beer drinker," he commented, as he took both cans from Michael.

"Dad, I'm twenty one in four days. What will be different in four days?" he questioned.

"You'll be four days older, and twenty one. Right now, you're twenty," his father responded with a firm tone.
"Honey…" their mom nudged. "It is a special occasion."

"Right, so what we doing here drinking beer? Where's the champagne?!" he remarked, standing sharply. Everyone followed as he went to go search for the champagne, leaving Courtney alone in the living room.

She got up and happened to notice that car was still sitting across the street. Courtney ignored it once again and went on upstairs to her room. She logged onto her computer, navigated to Facebook, and started a message.

Dad's home, wants you to come to dinner tomorrow. He wants to thank you. I'm so sorry! :P He's being super dweeby Dad atm.

Down in the kitchen, as Courtney's mom reached up to get the champagne flutes from the cabinet, she asked her husband, "Did you really have to invite that friend of hers over?"

"Aren't you just a bit curious how someone she met in less than five minutes knew more about our daughter than we did, and she lives in our home?" he replied.

"No, clearly you forgotten what it was like to be a teenager. We would be the last to know anything that is going on in our children's lives." She walked across the kitchen, as he popped the champagne bottle open and began to pour a glass for each of them.

Judging by the loud noise coming from the basement, it appeared Michael had returned to playing his video games. He was already back to playing Grand Theft Auto V on his Xbox One.

"Well, perhaps. However, whether we like it or not, this Lynn had a part in helping Courtney and saving her from that horrid boy. We know nothing about her, who she is or where she came from or why. Aren't you curious, dear?"–he paused to take a sip of his champagne–"All I am saying is we at least thank her and give her a chance to get to know us."

"…And for you to interrogate her?" his wife replied, with a hint of skepticism in her voice. He walked to the main room and felt his phone vibrate in his pocket. Pulling the phone out of the pocket, he didn't even look at the notification, but just opened up to the text screen and typed. Not now. I am doing as you instructed me to do. Be patient. He hit send, and returned the phone to his pocket.

"Don't worry, your phone will soon vibrate again, soon as you friends know you're back out. The Pressmans have organized a little party for us at the end of the week; I said I would get back to them. I didn't know if you'd be up for it," she explained while sitting down with her glass of champagne in hand.

"What? Oh, yes… erm… well," he stammered, clearly appearing distracted.

"Yes, you're right. Perhaps it is too much. I'll tell them to cancel," she stated.

"No, don't do that. I like to go out. That will be fine," he said firmly.

At the same time, back in her room, Courtney was gazing out her window and noticed someone got out of the Ford across the street. They began to approach the house.

"Who could that be?" Courtney's mom remarked, sounding surprised, as a double knock hammered on their front door.

"I'll go see," he said, as he got up and went to answer the door. Courtney ran to her bedroom door. She opened it slightly to eavesdrop on who was at the front door, just in time for her to hear her father declare, "No, thank you. We are not interested in buying into a bible subscription." He immediately closed the door, rather forcefully.

"Damn Jehovah's Witness. I wouldn't mind so much if it was the occasional Girl Scout. Least their bullshit taste good," her dad stated calmly.

Courtney closed her door and turned out the light. Her room was only highlighted by the glare of her computer monitor, as she ran over to the window to see the same person go back into the car. However, the car remained parked and did not drive away.

She noticed the person initially walked to the wrong side of the car. When they appeared to realize the mistake, they paused and walked around to the other side of the vehicle, the passenger side, and opened the door to get in.

Who doesn't know which side the passenger side of a car is on? she thought.

She returned to her computer, switched to safechat.com, and proceeded to send another message to Lynn.

I do not know what is going on, but there is something odd happening. A car arrived the same time as Dad and has not left. Someone from that car approached the house. Dad said it was a Jehovah's Witness. Then they returned to the car. I've never known them to drive dark grey Ford SUV's with tinted glasses before. Perhaps they're smartly dressed vampires? Anyway, watch your back when you come.

The next morning, she finally received a reply from Lynn, except it wasn't. It was next to Lynn's name, but the message had been written in third person.

Hi Courtney, this is Lola. Lynn is rather busy with a client, Mr. Hemlock, right now. However, she'd be glad to come over tonight. She will be off work around 10. Hope that is not too late.

Courtney informed her parents. They had been busy cleaning the house up, preparing as if this was some kind of family member coming to visit. Her dad seemed oddly nervous as well.

The grey Ford SUV was still parked across the street the next morning. She walked past it on her way to catch the bus into the city, but couldn't see inside it. She looked for the license plate as she walked by.

"Not police, it's a normal New York plate," she muttered under her breath.

Courtney never got a reply to her safechat.com message to Lynn, but she could tell the message had been read.

When she arrived back home later that day, she found the SUV still hadn't moved. She did not see anyone else ever leave the car, though she had to admit to herself that she wasn't watching the car the entire time. She had no way of knowing if the person she saw come to the house yesterday was still in the car or not.

Why would they be stalking her house? She didn't think they were watching her. *So why?*

The day went by fast. It was not too long before Courtney was in the living room with her parents awaiting Lynn's arrival.

"You said she be here at 11, right?" Courtney's dad questioned. She could hear the anxiety in his voice.

"Yeah, her boss told me she will be off work at 10, takes her 50 minutes to get here," Courtney replied.

"Where does she work?" her mom inquired.

"Some beauty shop. It's a summer job she does every summer; she worked there the last four years. During term time, she just works between college and on the weekends," she explained.

"So, what is she doing here?" her mum asked in response.

"Don't know. You can ask her yourself when she gets here," Courtney replied. She glanced at the clock, feeling rather annoyed.

"Ah, that must be her," her dad remarked, as they heard a car slowing down outside. However, when he got to the window to look out, the sound of the car had already sped back up and drove past their house.

"Oh, guess not. Somebody lost, no doubt. You did say she been here before?" He looked towards Courtney and his wife, who both answered with a nod.

Courtney felt her phone vibrate. It was Lynn. *Coming in the back door.*

"Dad, she said she is at the back door," Courtney reported, just as the knock came.

"Hello, I'm Lynn. Sorry I'm late, and for coming in the back. There is police out front and I didn't want to get mixed up with that. Looks like they pulled up a drunk driver outside your house?" Lynn said with a straight face, as she opened the door to let herself inside.

"What?" Courtney's dad remarked, with a tone of surprise in his voice. "There was nothing there just a moment ago," he commented, just as blue and red lights flashing began reflecting through the windows into the house.

"Come on in! Good to see you again!" Courtney greeted Lynn with a welcoming hug, while her dad stared at the strange car across the street with a worried look in his eyes.

"Well, come on in, dear. You must be starving. Hard day at work?" Courtney's mom attempted to make small talk.

"Yes, you could say I'm flushed," Lynn replied, as they all sat down at the main dining table to enjoy their late dinner.

8 CHAPTER EIGHT

"What the HELL you think you two were doing?!" Thunderous shouting rang out throughout that floor of the Police Precinct.

"Cap…" Sarah attempted to speak.

"SHUT THE HELL UP!! I'm talking here!" Howard slammed the door to his office shut.

Wilkinson and Sarah were standing in front of his desk.

"You follow an innocent man to his home, stalk his house for two days, and get the police put on you. Dumping me with the paperwork and fielding phone calls from the superintendent. And the head of the transit police shouting at me why they were not informed that I had operatives out in the field." He punched his desk, causing pictures to fall off his desk from the violent shake. "I couldn't even tell them why! Why? Because I was not fucking told!!"

"If you would let us explain," Wilkinson began.

"You are a guest of this department. You are new here; however, I suspect your captain would not tolerate this maverick type of antics. I told you, you are free to go after your perp as long as it doesn't interfere with the other cases we have on our desks.

"As for you, Sarah, I expected better from you. What the hell got into you?!" Howard was on a ranting rampage, trying to get in front of it would be like getting in the way of a runaway train.

"Sorry, Cap," she stated sharply.

This made Howard pause. *It's hard to argue when no one is arguing with you*, he thought. Howard turned and paced the floor, pushing his chair across the room and hitting the wall before he coming back to stand and stare out the window.

Wilkinson turned to look at Sarah, but for his efforts, all he received was a swift shake of her index finger, as Sarah indicated to him, "Not now!"

After five minutes of silence, Howard let out a heavy sigh and turned to face them.

"Okay... Tell me, so I can have an answer to tell my boss."

"We went to see the father before his release. We convinced him, as he was going to be a free man, and to atone for his crimes against the city, he should help us," Sarah started to explain.

"So you got him to turn informant? For what?" the Captain questioned. "What is his purpose?"

"We got the DA to agree to wipe out his record. Everyone looking over the case were all very upset about this particular case, to the point they want to use this case to promote a bill to change the law, so the DA was very willing," Sarah continued.

"Captain,"–Wilkinson took over the explanation–"Four years ago, he got arrested for defending his family. He killed that man, the boy who was dating his daughter. Going over the witness statements, Lynn, my suspect was there that night. What happened that night was her work, I'm sure of it. It is the same M.O. that happened in England. She was seen at Topshop earlier that day with the daughter."

"Right. So what has this to do with the dad and you stalking his house?" the Captain interrupted.

"We lost all trace of Lynn. We want the dad to be our eyes. We wanted him to bring Lynn to the house, so we could ID her and start tracing her," he explained.

"For what crime?" Howard asked.

"Captain?" Wilkinson replied to the Captain's question with one of his own.

"What did she do to warrant a trace?" Howard clarified his original question. "You cannot go following people you don't like just because you don't like them. Not unless the law changed in the last 12 hours. In which case, I need to go have a chat with my wife's boyfriend. However, you cannot touch this Lynn girl just because you *think* she committed a crime, no matter how it may look like her work. You need warrants for that here, probable cause," he explained. "Get used to that. You come to loathe that term."

He pointed to the chairs across from his desk. He recovered his own and they all sat down.

"Try to understand it from someone who does not know this perp, which fortunately, I am. You are saying four years ago, when she was new to the city and still 14, she managed to orchestrate a murder and not only does she not get her hands dirty, she manages to get someone else to do it leaving her completely in the clear?" He leaned back after presenting his point to allow Wilkinson the chance to refute it, if he could.

"Before she left, she was accused of stealing money from a shop. The person who reported the theft, she knew personally and had just given him oral. The money, I suspect, she took from the cash register. She planted it on one of her *friends*. That friend got caught with the money on her person.

"A week later, the person was found dead. Some of her male admirers were teaching the vic a lesson that went too far. Her friends were supposed to come and finish and beat her up; however, the vic died before they could. The entire situation was a clean-up. The person who reported the theft is doing time in HM Sandringham prison for statutory rape, molestation of a minor. Her friends and the boys would have all been arrested if the plan didn't get messed up, but thankfully it did," Wilkinson explained.

"Yes, so you've said before, I still have a hard time believing it; however, your Cap's signature to your case file is the only thing the adds any weight to this. Otherwise, your request would have been laughed back to Blighty.

"So, you think the murder of the boy four years ago is the same mistake as your last vic? Someone that got killed that she didn't want to kill?"

"At least not yet, or there and then," Wilkinson replied.

"So, who was it that spotted you and reported you to the transit police?" the

Captain questioned.

"There was a red car that slowed down, looking like it was going to stop, at 22:48. It then sped back up to normal speed and went by. There was a female driver of about 18 years of age. She looked at our direction, but no way she could have saw us," Wilkinson reported, before Sarah took over.

"The cop that arrived on scene said they got a call from a payphone across town," Sarah stated.

"Did you check...?" Howard was going suggest before Sarah interrupted him.

"Already did, Cap. They had someone go over while they were still talking to us. No one was at the phone, as expected; however, a shop across the street has a ATM. We called the bank and they gave the normal red tape. I got Patryk to put some FBI pressure on them and we will have the CCTV tape tomorrow by 9am."

"Alright, but you cannot simply go following someone until they commit a crime. You will have to wait for her to actually commit a crime. Don't worry, she will. I never fault your passion. Just apply it to something here.

"Sarah is behind her case load for the month; help her with her case. There was a homicide over on 3rd Avenue she was investigating. Oh, Sarah, should any ladies go for a morning walk, best to do it out of sight of gun range cameras. Reason I don't ask is because I don't have a reason to. Odd thing though, the instructor accidentally recorded last night's re-run of a Giants game over the tape." He winked toward Sarah.

"Thanks, Cap," she said with a small smile and a guilty expression on her face.

"Come on, Blue," she remarked, directing her attention to Wilkinson as they left the office.

"Blue?" he asked, sounding puzzled. "No longer 'runt'?"

"Yeah, you survived your first hazing from the Cap and you still have your shield. I decided to promote you from runt. First week academy grads often break at their first shouting and go be rent-a-cops or mall cops. You're still assigned to me, so now, we just need to pop your cherry, sweetheart. Don't worry, I'll be gentle on you. The streets won't!" she explained, with a smirk across her face, as they left the office.

"You know that was Lynn in that car, right?" Wilkinson attempted to protest.

"Ssh, you can't rush a girl. She needs time to make herself perfect for her man. She will come out of the bathroom in 5 minutes," Sarah mused, knowing the reference would fly over Wilkinson's head.

"Huh? What does that mean? I was talking about Lynn," he retorted, with a blank expression on his face

Men, Sarah thought. "You never been with a woman? Never had girlfriend?" Sarah asked.

"I'm not a virgin, if that is what you mean, but I never had a serious relationship outside of school," Wilkinson replied. They were heading down to the police station's vehicle garage again.

"You know DIY doesn't count, right, Blue?" Sarah teased. "How much did you pay her?" Seeing the expression on his face, she knew she was getting close to the truth.

"£40," he whimpered, clearly embarrassed. Sarah burst out laughing.

"Oh, Blue," she sighed. "How was it? Worth £40?"–Wilkinson shook his head–"Why are all boys so stupid? Man, your hormones must have had you by your balls. But you never had a real relationship? Ever?!" She didn't need to wait for him to answer, she already knew.

"No wonder you don't understand your perp," she remarked, as they got into the car. "I need to take you on a crash course on women."

The car sped out of the parking garage.

9 CHAPTER NINE

You have a request for assistance from your lost puppy. When you get back from your friend's, head over to my house. Lynn read the message while browsing her SafeChat app, but closed it when their food arrived to the table in front of her.

"Oh wow, it smells delicious," Lynn stated, as she caught a strong whiff of the steam billowing up from the serving plates into their nostrils.

"I thought I'd make you something to remind you of home," Courtney's mom said. Courtney smiled toward Lynn.

"Oh? What's that?" Lynn puzzled.

"Hotdogs and mash?" she prompted.

"You mean bangers and mash," she giggled. "Where's the ketchup?" Lynn eagerly awaited the moment she could dive into the meal. Courtney was the only one who knew this was one of Lynn's favorite dishes. Lynn didn't necessarily mind Courtney had apparently shared this little detail with her mom. Courtney continued to smile while she helped herself to the food.

"Why is it called bangers and mash?" asked Courtney's dad. He had been silent until then since the police arrived to deal with that DUI.

"Because the sausages you are supposed to use pop, sizzle, and bang in the oven as you take it out is how it got its name. Also, it used for Cricket teas. Sorry, Cricket dinners or lunches, as it holds references to the batter banging the ball and smashing it out of the stadium." Lynn explained, as she rapidly shoveled spoonful after spoonful into her mouth. An expression of joyful glee spread across her face as the taste hit her tongue.

"So how did you come to meet Courtney?" Courtney's dad inquired. No one appeared to notice him turn on his phone's voice recorder before returning the phone to his pocket.

"By chance, really. She was browsing in Top Shop and she needed a woman's opinion on a dress."–Lynn winked towards Courtney–"Her boyfriend was being a beast to her, so we convinced him to go off and be with his friends, which he clearly wanted, and invited Courtney to come with me and my guide on our personal shopping."

"Right. At 14, that is a little early to be out of school, right? Even for England?" Courtney's father continued the conversation.

"I graduated early. My brother was killed and I was taken advantage of by someone I thought I knew; there was too many emotional triggers and trauma to stay around there. My doctor at the time told me I had to get out if I was ever to heal, so my mother helped me get my study visa and I came to America to get a real education," Lynn explained. The room fell silent as Lynn finished her story.

"I'm sorry. How was he murdered?" he questioned.

"Dear!" his wife protested. Apparently, he'd gone too far with his interrogation.

"I would prefer not to talk about it. It's just, I left to get away from that, not relive it," Lynn replied solemnly.

"I'm sorry," he stated, as he received scathing looks from both his wife and daughter. They couldn't believe he was so forward with his questioning.

"Before you ask next, I came here that night because after the time at the shop, we had exchanged numbers and added each other to Facebook. Courtney was a new friend and I was new in the city. I was looking for a new friend and I had asked her out for a girls night out. She was going to show me around. My boss, Lola, lent me her car and her driver, who was going to take us to wherever she wanted to go and look after us for a special night of fun," Lynn explained with a sharp tone.

"I'm sorry for what happened to you. I'm sorry you had to be put in that position of having to need to defend your family. It was horrible that night." Skillful fake tears started to well up on que in Lynn's right eye as she recalled that dreadful night.

As Lynn bowed her head, Courtney's mom got up and hugged her tight, while shooting another disapproving expression toward her husband.

"I apologize to you, Lynn,"–he sat up straight in his seat–"I have been told my 'getting to know someone' can be like an interrogation. I wanted to invite you here tonight to thank you, not make you upset. You brought to our attention what was happening and going on with our daughter."–he reached over to grab Courtney's hand, emphasizing his point–"We as parents are often the last to know about anything going on with our kids, so the fact you told us when you did saved Courtney from getting hurt anymore. She would still be under his control now if it wasn't for you. You couldn't have helped what happened afterwards. You didn't make Tom come charging at you; that was his fault, not yours."

He stood up and walked around the table to stand next to Lynn and extended his hand.

"Again, I apologize, and as Courtney's Dad, thank you." He waited to see if Lynn would accept his handshake.

She sniffled a couple of times, and squeezed out of the Courtney's mom's hug. Lynn stood up and accepted the handshake. As she shook his hand, she noticed the glowing light from his pants pocket.

"Is it ok if Courtney and I head out now? I mean, thank you for the dinner; it was great." She turned to face Courtney's mother, the creator of tonight's meal, to show her appreciation. Then she turned back to face Courtney's father.

"Go on, then," he finally announced. Courtney stood up from the table.

"You mind if we go up to my room first, so I can get ready to head out?" she asked, looking puzzled. She did not recall having any plans to head out tonight, and suddenly, she felt worried she had forgotten making plans.

"Okay." Lynn smiled quickly, as Courtney's dad turned to walk back into the main room to watch TV while waiting for his food to digest. She lifted the iPhone very discreetly and placed it in her own pocket.

She quickly ascended the stairs. It was not long before the two girls were in Courtney's room. Lynn stayed by the door while Courtney was busy flinging clothes around the room trying to find something cute to wear.

Amidst the chaos, a random bra landed on top of Lynn's head. Trying to ignore it, she slowly removed it from her head and dropped it to the floor.

"When did you get a iPhone?" Courtney asked.

"Oh, it's just a temporary. I'm borrowing it for a moment," Lynn responded.

"Funny, looks like my Dad's. He wanted a Windows phone, but mom made him get that. He calls it a *Sesame Street* phone," Courtney continued, sounding distracted.

Lynn went into the Find My iPhone app on the phone, copied the details of Courtney's father's iCloud account, and sent them to her own phone. She locked the iPhone's screen again and returned it to her pocket.

"So, tell me about that car outside... what was it doing?" Lynn suddenly asked, causing Courtney to freeze in her place.

"Oh, so you did get my message. Good," she remarked, as she removed the 3rd pair of jeans she'd tried.

"I noticed the car pull up the same time as my dad arrived. I didn't see anyone get out as I closed the door. However, when I went upstairs, it was still there. I know it doesn't belong to anyone living next door," she stated. Courtney put on the top she finally decided to wear.

"You said someone got out of the car and came to the house?" Lynn asked next.

"Yeah, wearing a white shirt and black tie. He could have been a Jehovah's Witness by the way he was dressed, but they always walk. I never seen them use a car like that before." For the moment, Courtney had chosen to wear a short skirt instead of pants.

"Oh, there was one thing odd." She paused to look at Lynn.

"Hmm?" Lynn mused.

"On the way back to the car, he went to the wrong side. Who doesn't know

which side the passenger seat is on?" Courtney wondered.
"People not used to driving on the right side of the road," Lynn answered simply.

"Oh, true, I guess. It wasn't police though; it had normal NY plates," she commented.

"Do you remember the plate number?" Lynn asked, pulling her phone from her pocket.

"Yeah, 2 small letters saying PD, then 45784. It didn't say *Municipal* on it, so definitely not a city car," she recited, while Lynn jotted down the information.

"So, where we going?" Courtney asked, as she stood there ready to go.

Courtney had transformed. She ultimately decided on wearing a royal red Cupcakes and Cashmere top with 7 For All Mankind jeans that were torn with a patterned underlay. The outfit gave nothing away, except for bearing her shoulders. She had decided to forego the matching neck collar that went with the outfit.

"We will both know when we get there. Lola asked me to drop by her place after dinner. We can head over to hers, if you like, then head to someplace else." Lynn answered. Not waiting for a response, she turned and went down the stairs.

She went into the dining room, and bumped into Michael while he was collecting his dinner before returning to his GTA V game. He blushed instantly as soon as he saw her.

"Sorry," he said quickly, under his breath.

"Heya, it's okay," she responded, pushing the left side of her hair back and tilting her head to the side. "Getting food?" she asked.

"No... er, I mean, yeah," he stuttered.

"Be careful with those hotdogs. You can choke on long objects going down, all the way down your throat until they explode in your mouth." She gestured with a closed fist to her mouth.

"Erm. Right, thanks." He ran off quickly, while Lynn laughed at how she had taunted him so successfully.

Courtney had gone into the main room where her parents were watching television. With Michael gone, Lynn placed Courtney's dad's phone on the floor, then stood back up and waited by the door.

After a couple of minutes, Courtney returned to the dining room, followed by her dad.

"Okay, let's go," Courtney announced.

"Please be back at 2am please; I wish to lock the door by then. If you not going to make it or sleep over at Lynn's, please call to let me know," her dad instructed, patting his pocket for his phone. He realized it wasn't there and patted the other pocket before quickly looking around the room. He found it lying on the floor next to his chair at the dining table.

"Damn phone. I'm always losing this stupid thing."–he looked up–"Go on, be safe," he said, as he waved them out the door.

"I tell you, Lynn, your iPhone looks almost exactly like my dad's," Courtney commented a moment later.

"They do make more than one of the same color, you know?" Lynn teased.

"Yeah, I guess."–Courtney paused–"So why does Lola want you to come over?"

"You remember the lost puppy the other day?"–Lynn looked toward Courtney as they got into Lynn's car–"He apparently reached out to me for assistance."

"You going to help him?" Courtney questioned.

"I'll have to see first what he wants," she replied, as they drove off into the night.

It was just a short drive to Lola's over on 169th street in Queens, NY. Lola lived practically next door to a cemetery and golf course, and wasn't too far from the college. Lola said it was so she could always keep an eye on fashion; the young will always be first to start or change a fashion trend. It was her way of staying ahead of the curve.

It was almost 1am by the time they got to Lola's. Lynn pulled up outside in front of Lola's door. Lola opened the door to greet them, and found Lynn had brought company.

"Welcome, Courtney," Lola greeted her.

"I hope you don't mind me bringing her. I thought we could head out after we were done here. She was telling me some interesting things about Jehovah's Witnesses upgrading to Ford SUV's now," Lynn announced, as she got out of the car and manually locked the door with the car key. "She even got us a plate number."

"Oh, really? No, I don't mind. I appreciate the company." Lola stepped back to allow Lynn and Courtney to ascend the stoop and enter her home.

Lynn passed her phone to Lola.

"You guys want anything to drink?" Lola offered.

"No, we are fine, just ate not too long ago," Courtney replied.

"Oh, that's right! What did you have to eat?" Lola continued.

"My favorite, bangers and mash," Lynn chimed in. "Apparently, they wanted to remind me of home." She smiled softly toward Courtney.

"Well, that's funny, because your lost puppy reached out to you for help." Lola walked over with her laptop open and laid it on Lynn's lap for her to look at the screen display of her Facebook account.

"I think you need to tell me a little more about him. Is this going to be a problem?"–Lola gave Lynn a serious look– "I mean, is he going to let you go again after you help him?"

"*If* I help him," Lynn corrected.

"Oh, please!" Lola remarked dismissively. "You've already decided to help."

"What? How do you know?" Lynn asked, sounding surprised.

"Because you are now interested in who the *she* is, and who he has replaced you with. It was obvious on your face soon as you read it," Lola stated while glancing sideways toward Courtney.

"Why would she care who he has replaced Lynn with? She is over here now. They're 9000 miles apart," Courtney remarked, taking her cue. "She doesn't even care about him, not like that anyway."

"Do you think I should talk to him? It doesn't hurt to see what he has to say." Lynn pointed out, dodging Courtney's question. "We don't even know what he needs help with. It may be nothing I can help with, then I risk exposing myself for nothing. It's what, 6 in the morning over there now, almost 7? You even think he will be up?"

"Why don't I talk to him for you?" Courtney proposed. Lola and Lynn looked at each other. There was small hint of a smile from Lola.

"What do you mean?" Lola questioned. "Why would you want to talk to him?"

"Well, Lynn doesn't want to expose herself to him, and she said earlier tonight, she doesn't want to rehash her past understandably. He would have had to of seen I'm on your friends list, so why not let me be your pee guard?"

"Pee guard?" Lynn asked, with a puzzled look on her face.

"You call him your lost puppy and puppies pee everywhere, so you put a guard up to protect your furniture and such. They're called puppy pee guards. Like mud flaps, but for pee," Courtney explained.

"I don't know about you talking to him though," Lynn bounced back.

"Oh, come on, it makes perfect sense. Like you said, doesn't hurt to just talk, I can say no to him and no harm will be done," Courtney reasoned. "I owe you; let me do this for you!"

"Well, I don't think we can refuse an offer like that." Lola stood up, having obvious difficulty suppressing a smile.

Courtney ran over and sat next to Lynn. Taking control of the laptop, she got Chris' information, then opened a separate browser. Courtney kept Lynn's account open in Chrome, while she used Firefox to log into her own account. Then she opened the messenger.

"Should I tell him to use SafeChats or just keep it on here?"

"Keep it simple. Keep it on Facebook until we know what is going on first,"

Lola instructed, sounding more serious now.

Courtney started typing.

Hi, Chris. This is Courtney, friend to Lynn. We saw your message. What is going on? Please accept this invite to chat.

She took a deep breath. As she exhaled, she hit send. Next, all they could do was wait to see if the chat invite would be accepted.

978-0692579237 (C B Bartram Books)

10 CHAPTER TEN

Detective Sarah pulled up at Prospect Park in Brooklyn. Sharply, she pulled over across traffic into a parking spot, with the sound of honking car horns surrounding the vehicle.

"I'm surprised no one wears out their horns in this city," Wilkinson observed.

"Oh, it's worse over on the other side of the Hudson," she replied, as she switched the engine off. "You know why you're here?"

"Well, I assume it isn't you showing me around the city, so to investigate that homicide case the Captain told us to go work on?" Wilkinson responded, looking around the area they were in. It looked like any other street in the city, crowded and bustling with both cars and foot traffic. He noticed a couple of people going into the #1 Garden shop.

"We here to eat Chinese? Ironic name, kind of," Wilkinson chuckled.

"Maybe if you pass, Blue, I'll buy you Chinese; however, no. Come on," she stated, as she got out of the car, followed by Wilkinson. "Why do you think it's ironic?"

"Calling a shop after a garden in the one place where there is perhaps the least grass in the world maybe," Wilkinson answered, while he began to walk around the area.

"Ah, Blue, such a rookie. Come. I told you, you need a crash course in training on women. You will never be able to catch your perp until you understand her."–Sarah started walking–"We don't have time to wait another

10 years for what you should have learned going through your 20s."

She picked up her pace and Wilkinson followed closely.

"Take off your tie," she shouted back at him. "Just do it." She knew he wanted to ask why.

She walked down past the #1 Garden to the corner of the block. Then she stopped and looked back at Blue.

"Bit early, isn't it?" Wilkinson commented.

Sarah pushed the door open to Farrell's Bar, a nice looking watering hole with glass windows, a corner-facing door, and an American flag propped against the window. The frame of the bar's door and windows looked like oak wood. Who knows? Maybe it was. The bar had been in business since before the second World War.

Farrell's had one long counter and multiple side booths. No food was served here; it was just a place to go after a hard day's work that you just want to forget. There were smart TVs lining the walls showing various sports games: hockey, baseball, football, golf, you name it. Above the booths, mirrors spanned the walls. Ceiling fans kept the overheated bar cool, but not too cool. Cold men don't need drinks; heat makes a man thirsty. There's nothing better than an ice cold, thirst quenching craft beer from the tap.

"Sa…hic…rah!!" a bar patron drunkenly bellowed, as she opened the door wide. "What the blazing? Who's the kid? Oh! Hi, Sarah! When did you get… hic… here?"

The man was overweight, easily at 220lbs, with a bald spot atop his head of short black hair. A jacket hung on the back of his chair, while four to six empty beer glasses sat on the table in front of him. A full glass also sat on the table, waiting for him to finish the glass he held in his hand. Wilkinson saw the gold NYPD shield attached to his belt. He was in one of the side booths.

There was another man sitting at the counter, drinking a Coor's. This one, Wilkinson noticed, was a sergeant of the traffic division.

Wilkinson, only seeing places like this on Law & Order: SVU or NYPD Blue, couldn't help but feel kind of impressed and awed by it. However, he also felt kind of embarrassed at the sight of some the drunks. There were no other words to describe it.

"Don't judge, Blue. Not yet," Sarah said flatly. "GENTLEMEN!" Sarah started to announce, getting everyone's attention. "My partner here, Blue, is rather new, not just to the city, but to women. He needs to learn, and fast. Now, I am going to walk over to the bar, and suddenly become so engaged in my ice cold Coke, while munching on bar peanuts and watching that exciting rerun of yesterday's game, that I am suddenly going to become deaf to any conversation going on here. You need to tell him all you know about women. I'm going to be generous and give you all of 5 minutes." She walked over, pulled out her *Lady* and placed it on the counter, intimidating all who saw it.

"Your time starts, gentlemen,"–she paused to sit down on a bar stool– "...now."

Wilkinson just stood there as he was forced to witness Sarah's speech. Suddenly, he was pulled down into an empty seat by the drunkard they passed as they came into the bar. The man sitting at the counter began to walk toward their booth.

"So, what do you need to know?" the Sergeant from the counter began.

"Sarah says I need a crash course, so I guess, assume everything," Wilkinson replied earnestly.

"All women are bitches," the drunkard suddenly blurted out. "All they do is steal your heart, your house, your money, your cat, take your kids and hold you hostage by your balls."–he sighed–"Never trust them, any of them. Fuck 'em, but never give them a key to your home."

"Women can be a bit demanding," the sergeant chimed in with a chuckle.

"Sarah said something about my perp, that she will be 5 minutes. I don't understand what she means," Wilkinson remembered.

"She means 20 minutes to an hour more like it. Boy, you really are green to women. You even get to touch a pussy yet? Or you some kind of 40-year-pussy?" the sergeant questioned.

"Hmm... pussy, nice big boobs, nice firm ass, and pink lips will do me just fine," he mused. "You can keep the mind and mouth that comes with it. Women just love to toy with you and play with your heartstrings. Make you fall in love with them 'cause they just want everyone to be friends. They break your heart by crushing it with their heels, then ask you to be their friends as if nothing they did mattered."

"Even women like Sarah?" Wilkinson asked next.

They all turned to look at her, and they both nodded to him.

"You've seen her ass you followed enough, haven't you?"

"Man, he wouldn't know what he is looking at. He's too green," the drunkard interjected sharply.

"Why do you do that? Objectify women like that?" Wilkinson asked defensively, not taking too kindly to what they just did with his partner.

"They do it to us too. It's okay to look and dream, just not ok to actually do it, unless they say yes, of course," the sergeant remarked, picking up the conversation. "How old is your perp?"

"18," Wilkinson responded, passing the photo to them.

"OH MAN! SNAP, FAPPING MATERIAL! DAMN!" the drunkard burst out. "Hey, when you're done with her, give me a call. I wouldn't mind 5 minutes alone with her," he laughed.

"She's young, so she isn't going to care too much. She doesn't have experience in life yet. She be full of herself, ambitious, money, and power hungry, very flirty. That's women's main weapon, you see. They know you want to fuck 'em and they use that against us men. Even your partner, Sarah. You honestly haven't thought about hitting that?" he asked Wilkinson honestly.

"No, she's my friend and partner," Wilkinson replied defensively. The two men both raised their glasses to their mouths to take another drink.

BANG! The sound of the Desert Eagle rang through the bar, as a bullet had just been shot straight through both of the men's glasses before they were able to take a sip. The bullet was embedded in the wall beside them.

"Times up!" Sarah stood up and laid a couple of Franklins on the counter. "For the glasses and hole in the wall," she noted to the bartender.

"Go home, boys. You've had enough! Come on, Blue. You passed," she

stated, as she walked straight past Wilkinson and out of the bar.
Sarah waited until she was on the sidewalk before she stopped and turned to wait for her partner to catch up with her.

As he walked up to her, she quickly leaned in and kissed him on the cheek.

"You're sweet, but innocent. Come, I promised you Chinese." She started to walk off toward #1 Garden.

"Wait, you mind telling me what that was all about?"–he pulled her back– "What that was about?" he demanded, pointing to his cheek.

"You need to learn about women. You need an honest experience, including the ideas those naïve, dumb, pig-headed, dumb males have about women. You need to hear both sides. You've just heard the male view of women; drunk people tell no lies. And that..."–she pointed to his cheek–"If you don't know, then I guess that will be something you will always be wondering about," she mused, with a smile.

"Now, come. You got me graving Chinese. I do love me some wontons. After we eat, I'll take you to the second lesson."

She turned as they headed off to the #1 Garden Chinese restaurant.

11 CHAPTER ELEVEN

"I called her mom, told her she will be sleeping over," Lola noted, as she entered the room and looked over at the passed out Courtney laying limp over to the side. "I also did what you said: called the dad's phone, let it ring twice, and hung up."

Lola walked across the room and sat in the chair opposite Lynn. Lynn was working on a laptop, with a second laptop sitting to her right. This second laptop had Courtney's Facebook account open on the screen.

"Why did you have me sedate her?" Lola questioned, as she discarded a small syringe on the coffee table.

"How long will she be out for?" Lynn asked, ignoring Lola's question.

"She will be out until morning," Lola stated, as she looked over at the laptop to Lynn's side. "What's going on? Has your puppy replied?" Lola pushed, curiously.

Lynn quickly glanced at Courtney and poked her in the ribs to make sure she was really out, not faking it.

"Her father was followed home from prison. The plate number is registered to a female detective working at the same police station as my friend from England. I don't think that is a coincidence. The person that came to door, I believe it was him."

"Your... *friend?*" Lola retorted, making air quotes with her hands.

"It would make sense; however, I believe they following him not to watch him, but to get at me. She is unaware," Lynn sighed. "She has become somewhat of a liability to me. Her dad was recording our conversation. The glow from his phone screen illuminated from within his pants pocket." Lynn returned to typing on the laptop in her lap, while briefly taking a sideward glance at the second laptop. There was no reply from Chris yet.

"So, you think her dad is working for them, but why? You haven't done anything here. What is your plan? Why not just delete the recording?" Lola suggested.

"Because I plan to become the hunter, not the hunted. I got his iCloud details from his phone. I just went onto the iCloud app and logged in. I'm keeping an eye on his location. While you called his phone, I traced the signal pinning his phone. I was able track the echo requests bouncing back to your phone from his, retrieved his IP address supplied by his service provider–not his personal wifi–plus his SIM digital signal code."

Lola stared blankly at Lynn.

"Meaning I'm pinning his phone and running a continuous trace, as well as keeping track via the Apple app to know where he is going." Lynn clapped her hands suddenly.

"Got him!"–she grabbed some paper and wrote down the location– "Typical."

"What's typical?" Lola wondered.

"Looks like I'm going to be the best girlfriend ever. The place her father is going to give that recording to my friend… Well, he just got out of prison. I'm sure you don't have to think too much of what men miss most in prison," Lynn explained, as Lola rolled her eyes.

"Okay, so why do you have to go? You're risking a lot; you've gone to a lot of trouble to stay low and out of sight. Why risk it now?"

Lynn stood up, and quickly texted to her contact "Boyfriend." *Be ready in 10 mins. I'm taking you for some fun!*

"Relax. Just think of it like this, I been given my two cards, and I just want to see the flop," Lynn explained, as she pointed to the laptop and then Courtney. "You're a good teacher. Can you watch her? And also the laptop in case he replies?" she asked.

"Sure," Lola replied. Lynn readied herself, and started heading toward the exit.

"Tomorrow, when she wakes up, bring her with you to work. Give her a free transformation." Lynn's voice faded as she continued to walk farther and farther away.

"Why? Transform to what?" Lola inquired.

"To look close enough to look like me," Lynn shouted, as the door shut behind her.

It took Lynn just five minutes to drive over to her boyfriend's house in Queens, NY.

"Hi, get in," Lynn instructed, as she pulled up outside his home. "We don't have a lot of time, sweetie. Place closes at 4 and it's already approaching 2."

Her boyfriend named Andi was wearing dress pants called Black Popper Joggers, and some kind of kickers that looked posh, but stopped short of being true dress shoes. He also wore a grey zip through denim jacket over top of a white and black speckled short sleeve dress shirt.

He was decked out in accessories too, including a quartz watch and some kind of pendant. Lynn recognized it was a locket, but she did not know the significance of it. He had short military-style crew cut hair, and stood 6'2" tall. He was taller than Lynn, which she really liked. She always imagined being picked up by a handsome man and swept off her feet. He had a couple of facial scars, but she never pried to learn about their origins.

They had been dating since last year, though Lynn kept him at a distance. She told him she wanted to wait until she turned eighteen, which has happened now. She was starting to run out of excuses. Tonight, she planned to give him just a little of what he desired, just enough to keep him hooked on her.

The man came running around the front of the car and jumped inside. Not waiting for him to get settled, she sped off. It was another eight minutes before she took the exit 12B onto I-495 and they finally started chatting. Lynn turned to him, quickly looking him up and down.

"I got you some singles for tonight. It's on me, just don't spend it all at once," she remarked, as she held up a wad of singles. Two hundred, to be exact.

"What? We going to a strip club?" he laughed, thinking she was joking with him.

"It doesn't always have to be your friends that take you. I know how men work and I appreciate that you are waiting for me before we take it seriously. However, I know you have needs too, and I figured you cannot touch the girls. Doesn't mean I couldn't give you a hand..." she mused, as a smile spread across her face.

"You serious? This isn't a joke?" He felt very hesitant, not knowing if this was some sort of trick or if his girlfriend testing him.

"Like I said, I know men," Lynn explained simply. She leaned over and kissed him, causing the car to swerve a little, as she was going 80mph on the interstate. Several horns blared at her as a reward.

"So, which one we going too?" he questioned.

"Pumps."

"Oh, this is going to be good," he remarked, with a tone of excitement filling his voice.

"Oh yes, it is. It is going to be a night of fun for both of us," Lynn mused, staring ahead through the windshield.

.

12 CHAPTER TWELVE

"Okay, is this where you are going to get my cherry popped? Or do you need to cash a check?" Wilkinson joked, looking out the window. To his right, he saw a check cashing facility. Attached to the adjoining building, also on his right, slightly behind him and Sarah, was a little grill place called Manny's Grill. A sign claimed they served breakfast to lunch.

Sarah turned the car right and pulled up next to the building behind the check-cashing place. She stopped underneath an advertising board, which currently displayed an advert for whiskey.

"I'm still full from the Chinese earlier," Wilkinson continued, as he noticed the time on the car's clock flip to 23:55.

Sarah switched off the car engine and unfastened her seatbelt. Wilkinson was about to open his door to get out of the car, but Sarah quickly pressed the button to lock the car doors to prevent him from getting out of the vehicle. She opened the divider between the front seats and pulled out a thermal flask container. She removed the lid and filled the cap with its contents.

"Here, drink this. It will be the only drink you will have tonight. You understand?" She gazed at him with a serious expression.

"What is it?" he asked hesitantly, as he took the cap in his hand and sniffed it.

"Jameson Whiskey. Just drink it, I'll explain after," Sarah instructed, while staring him down until he drank it all.

"You could've given me an ice cube," he remarked. The burning effect took hold as he downed the whiskey.

"Whiskey is meant to be drank neat," she retorted. She refilled the cap and downed it in one gulp.

"Ahh!" Sarah gasped, swallowing and shaking her head. She too felt the burn of the whiskey in her throat. She replaced the cap and put it back in the divider between the two front seats.

Sarah reached over to remove Wilkinson's tie. Then she snapped off two buttons from the top of his shirt to bare his chest.

"Easy, Blue," Sarah commented, as she could tell he was getting excited. "If I wanted you, you would know. I am just making sure you don't get us or you killed tonight." She grabbed his shield off his shirt and shoved it inside his sock, down into his shoe.

"Keep your jacket off," she instructed. As he removed his jacket, she undid a few of the buttons on her shirt to allow her bust to fill out a bit. She reached over Wilkinson and into the glove box to pull out a bra.

Sensing what was going to happen next, Wilkinson decided to become very interested in what was currently outside his car window.

"So, explain," he demanded.

"Like I said, Blue, you're sweet," Sarah stated with a smile. She reached under her shirt and unclipped the gun holster, letting it fall to her lap. She then unhooked the front clasp of her bra, pulled off the straps to remove that bra, and put it into the glove box.

"We will be doing a lot here tonight. Grand Street don't take too kindly to police, so I gave you a drink, so you don't smell like a cop. The buzz will hit you in 15 and wear off after 30," Sarah explained. She now began the reverse process and slipped on the new padded pushup bra.

"It is okay, you can look. You're not going to be able to see anything." Wilkinson turned to look at Sarah.

He saw her slide the new bra up her shirt, then saw the right strap come out of her right shirtsleeve, slide over her hand, and back up to her shoulder. She did the same with the left side to the other side, then clasped the bra.

With the new bra pushing up Sarah's breasts, her bust appeared to expand under the buttons she just undid. She was displaying much more cleavage, making it appear as though her breasts had grown two cup sizes.

"Impressive," he remarked.

"We have a lot to do here; all this will be your second lesson on women." She finished adjusting her shirt before she continued.

"This will be the women's version on women. We also will be meeting our informant. He called saying he met with her and recorded their conversation. I will also be working my case. The lead I got at the bar pointed my perp is going to be here tonight, so I told our informant to come here. Figured I could multi-task and get your lesson, help you with your perp, and get my perp in one lesson. There is just one thing…" she reported, as her voice trailed off.

She got out the flask again and gave him another drink.

"Your blood in your brain is going to leave and go straight to your head. I'm banking on you being green. You won't be as bad as most men." Sarah unlocked the car and stepped out, followed by Wilkinson.

"Aren't you overdoing it for a grill?" he questioned, as she started to walk the opposite way, away from the grill. She continued around the corner past the check-cashing place and stopped. Wilkinson bumped into her.

"We aren't going to no grill. Happy birthday!" she exclaimed, pointing.

Wilkinson followed her finger to a sign hanging on the same building, but at the opposite end from the grill.

"Just which cherry were you referring too, again?" Wilkinson stood there with his mouth gaping, as the meaning of the sign sunk into his brain. His head quickly snapped around, as he noticed the nearly naked woman standing out front next to the bouncer.

"…and there goes the blood. That was fast," she remarked, shaking her head and rolling her eyes. "*Men*! Come on, Blue." She pulled him by his belt to get him moving, or else he would have been standing there staring at that woman forever.

Sarah and Wilkinson walked up level with the doorman.

"You must be freezing." Sarah winked to the girl and tipped her an Andrew, as the doorman began the normal pat down.

"You have no idea. Who's your cute friend?" she questioned, nodding in Blue's direction.

The doorman, finished with Sarah, started the pat down on Wilkinson next.

"Hi, I am, erm… erm…" Wilkinson blubbered, apparently unable to say his own name, while staring at her nipple covers shaped like US flags. If it wasn't for them, she would be completely topless.

"Well, erm, nice to meet you. Hope you have a nice time tonight," she mused, smiling.

"Urgh, sorry about him. He's green," Sarah apologized, as she shook her head. "Blue, if you are done drooling, pick up your tongue and come on."

"It's okay; I'm used to it. Enjoy tonight," the girl giggled. Suddenly, Wilkinson found his tongue.

"Hey, Sarah, do you like…?" Wilkinson started, before Sarah suddenly stopped, turned, and stepped up very close in front of him.

"You better not finish that question, Blue. We all had the college phase. Well, most of us did. So, you keep that thought in your head as a fantasy, but never *ever* try to put it into words again. Get it?" she threatened, turning sharply. To avoid wasting any more time, she pulled him along behind her to make sure he actually came into the club, instead of staring at the girl outside the door all night.

It was not long before that girl was out of his mind altogether as he now stood before a bar surrounding three poles with very lovely nubile ladies dancing. Loud music blasted through the club. Pump It by the Black Eyed Peas started playing just after midnight.

All the walls around the club were covered in mirrors, and there were seats spanning the counter of the bar with seats on the sides. Deep dark blue and red mood lighting illuminated the club, while bright spotlights were focused on the ladies. This was Pumps, an exotic dancing club.

The sound of the stage announcer blasted through the club with another girl's name as the three original girls walked off the stage. Blue felt miles away as he took in the entire scene. His mind was a million miles away, as he saw the waitresses walking around to the tables serving drinks.

"You've never been to a club before?" Sarah inquired. She didn't get a verbal response; seeing Blue's gaping mouth gave her the answer she needed.

"Come on, Blue," Sarah laughed. She took his hand, directed him over to the counter, found him a seat, and propped him onto the chair.

"It's okay, Blue. You enjoy yourself for now." Sarah sat down in the chair next to Wilkinson.

The bartender approached Sarah. He was a fairly short man at about 5'6" tall, and had a slight goatee beard that appeared to have just started to grow. His hair reached back to the collar of his black T-shirt, which displayed the Pump's logo of a circle with two silhouetted women dancing on a pole.

"What you having, love?" he asked.

"Strawberry daiquiri, no olive please," Sarah replied.

"For him?" He nodded towards Blue.

"Besides a drool bucket, give him a Heineken," Sarah ordered.

Blue was still hypnotized by the woman on stage. The woman on the pole directly in front of him had just lifted herself up to the top of the pole. With the pole held firmly in place between her legs and into her crotch, she extended her left leg out straight. Leaning back to support herself with just her left hand on the pole, she spun around 360 degrees and landed on the stage with both legs facing Blue. She quickly spread her legs and thrust up towards him.

"So, what color are her eyes, Blue?" Sarah asked jokingly.

"Huh?" Blue replied. Sarah let out a big chuckle in response. The bartender promptly returned with her daiquiri and placed the bottle of Heineken in front of Wilkinson.

"First time?" the bartender suspected. Sarah nodded. The bartender smiled and quickly glanced at Blue again.

The woman swung clockwise around the pole holding herself. Then, she pushed up off the ground and cartwheeled backwards. Once she was upside down, she pushed herself all the way to the top allowing her feet to touch the ceiling. She wrapped her body around the pole and slid down slowly. Half way down, her panties dropped on the stage, just inches away from Blue. However, Blue completely missed it because of how completely mesmerized he was by her. It was as if they were the only two people in the room. For the final move of her act, her breasts hit the floor as she descended from the pole to lie on her chest.

Suddenly, Blue started clapping, while the DJ started to announce the next act. The song My Humps by the Black Eyed Peas started blasting throughout the club.

"Hey! Chenelle!" the bartender hollered to the girl who had just concluded her act. Once she looked over, he quickly pointed towards Blue.

"He's a freshman," the bartender commented. The girl jumped down off the stage to allow the next dancer to take her place. She smiled and walked up to Blue.

"Hey, honey," she remarked seductively, as she passed Blue. She reached out to touch Sarah's hand tenderly. Sarah gingerly pulled her over in response, and the two kissed passionately as Sarah held on to the back of Chenelle's neck. The kiss was brief, but long enough to leave Wilkinson with a mental image he would never forget.

"Hey, honey, enjoy your time here."–Chenelle winked as she dropped her panties in front of him–"You can give these back if you want a private dance later. Bring your friend." She gave Blue a quick kiss on the cheek and walked off.

"Not a word, Blue," Sarah insisted, blushing. "One more dance, then we need to work."

Blue started to raise the bottle, but quickly stopped and set it back down.

"Just hold it, Blue. Keep those hands where I can see them now," Sarah remarked, halfway joking.

She glanced at the brunette girl who just started her act, and found she was wearing a clumsy plaid schoolgirl outfit. Sarah looked down at the time on her cellphone, which read 00:45.

"I'm going to the girl's room. You be okay here? Remember, don't drink, just keep holding the bottle." Blue was too distracted to fully comprehend Sarah's instructions. Sarah sighed and grabbed his crotch tightly to get his attention. "Do NOT DRINK! You understand me?" Sarah demanded.

"Yeah," he responded. Blue nodded as well, but quickly turned his attention back to the woman on stage.

Sarah knew she had gotten the best answer she was going to get from him in this state. Satisfied, Sarah walked off around the bar toward the restroom. Blue watched her black silhouette vanish on the other side of the bar to his left, but he did not care. His attention was completely focused on Jeanette.

~

A car pulled up to the sidewalk over on Grand Street. The passenger side of the windshield bore the Lyft logo. The rear passenger door opened, as a man emerged from the back seat.

"Thanks," he said, as he closed the door, watched the car drive away, and checked his cellphone. *Yep, this is the place.* He put his phone back into his pants pocket and proceeded toward the entrance of Pumps.

He ignored the woman, and just raised his arms to allow the doorman to do his thing. He kept looking around nervously.

"Has a man and woman come in tonight?" he asked the bouncer.

"You know how many people come here in a night? You need to be more descriptive than that," the bouncer retorted.

"Err, never mind." He made his way inside the club. The song My Humps was already playing when he entered, and Jeanette, his favorite dancer, was on stage. He headed over to the bar, where he saw one guy sitting at the bar holding a drink. He decided to give him some space and took the 4th seat down. Little did he know, this man at the bar was Wilkinson.

"What you having?" the bartender inquired, as he took his seat.

"Normal, and Jeanette's number," the man proposed.

"Alright, one IPA, and you know I can't do that, but you could ask her in a private session. You want me to ask her?"

Jeanette just completed a counter-clockwise spin on the pole, and slid towards the guy holding his beer. She ripped apart her shirt, revealing her bra as the only thing covering her upper body. She stepped back, tilted her head to the left, and latched herself back onto the pole. Upon spotting her number one customer, he became her focus.

"You can let her work," the man stated simply.

"Sure enough," the bartender replied, smiling.

While slowly shaking her hips, she slowly stepped around the pole. Her hands continually caressed herself up and down, as she repetitively extended her ass out to this man.

He started to drink his beer, and his eyes met with Jeanette's lovely eyes. She made a tiny thrust movement toward him, and slightly lifted up the front of the skirt to reveal the white laced panties she wore underneath, playing to her role of a naughty schoolgirl. The school tie hung between her breasts.

The man threw $5 onto the stage in her direction, making sure Jeanette kept her attention on him. This caught Wilkinson's attention. He appeared to get annoyed watching her go over to the other man, where she squatted down in front of him and she spread her legs wide open. As she stood up, she leaned forward to shove his head between her breasts and shook them over his face. She felt him bite onto her bra, so she took the opportunity to unclasp it from the back. When she stood up, the bra fell away from her body, revealing her naked breasts to everyone watching.

She immediately stepped back and returned to the pole. Wilkinson threw in $5 now to get Jeanette's attention. He was annoyed about not being able to see when her bra fell off, revealing her breasts, and he felt jealous that the other man got to see before him. Then Jeanette picked herself up and spun around again.

Leading up to the climax of her act, towards the end of the song, she landed on the stage again. She kicked off her panties, and let them land on the stage. She spun around once more, and using gravity in her favor, she allowed her skirt to fly up showing everyone underneath. She landed just as the song finished.

"Nice performance," Sarah remarked from backstage, clapping as Jeanette made her way off the stage.

"Thanks," she replied, looking curiously at Sarah as she headed into the changing rooms.

"Pity the other guy didn't come in sooner. You had them baited," Sarah commented.

"Yeah, but I'm not worried. That guy always wants a dance from me; I think he's in love with me or something," Jeanette answered, looking confused. "Sorry, are you new?"

"You can say that," Sarah replied, as the next act walked passed her. She looked out past the curtain to find Blue was still at the bar. "Good boy," she muttered under her breath.

"When he asks you for that dance, find me. I will be joining you." Sarah slipped her a fifty, but Jeanette pushed back.

"You don't need to tip. Dancing with another girl is always fun. Any particular reason?" She waved Sarah into the changing room with her.

The room wasn't too big and contained various lockers. Sarah noticed the other woman who had kissed her earlier, Chenelle, entered the room shortly after she and Jeanette. As Chenelle walked in, she gave Sarah wink.

"Hey, honey, couldn't get enough, huh?" Another woman walked by to start getting changed, presumably to ready herself for the next act.

"You know it."–Sarah smiled–"Could you look after my friend? Make sure he doesn't get into trouble out there."

"Oh, sure. No worries. I meant it about the dance though. I'd dance for you for free," Chenelle mused, blowing an air kiss.

"Okay, you peak my curiosity, so explain," Jeanette stated, as she patted the seat next to her, inviting Sarah to sit down next to her.

Back in the main room, Blue was enjoying the next act. The other guy had been completely forgotten and ignored.

"Hey, so you planning on mounting those or returning them?" a female voice teased, snapping Blue out of his trance. "It's not polite to just stare; you should tip the lady."

Blue instantly got a dollar out of his pocket and tipped the new girl on stage.

"So, you going to buy me a drink?" Chenelle questioned, as she sat down next to Blue. "Be a good boy and tip her good. She has a living to make."

~

A red '96 Dodge Stratus slowly came around the corner on Grand Street past the Grill. Lynn noticed a Ford with tinted windows parked there. She decided to go slow until she could read the plate and ultimately chose to park right next to it.

As Lynn turned the engine off, she quickly checked her cellphone. The Find My iPhone app was open on her phone, displaying the location of Courtney's dad's iPhone, which happened to be just a few feet away.

"Well, come on then! You excited?" she exclaimed, while looking toward her boyfriend.

"I still cannot believe you're doing this. Still not sure this isn't some sort of test," he answered with a skeptical tone, as they both got out of the car.

"Well, I will get to see if I am really your type, or what type of woman really gets you excited?" Lynn smiled, and gave his hand a quick squeeze. "It is okay. Some girls may get jealous, but I recently learned you cannot fight nature. You're going to look at other women, if you admit it or not to me."

As soon as they turned the corner, his focus centered right on the woman standing out front.

"My case in point. It's okay! She is very nice." Lynn hinted, "I see why they are using her to entice men into the club. Just remember one thing, sweetie." She stopped and grabbed both of his hands to force him to look directly at her.

"None of these women will, or ever will, love you. That is the ploy of these places. They make you fall in love with them. Please be better than that, okay?" She kissed him.

Not waiting for an answer, as she didn't have much faith in him, Lynn pulled on his hands and they resumed walking to entrance.

"Hey, sweetie, nice flags," Lynn laughed, as the bouncer started the pat down on her boyfriend.

"Have a good time you two," the woman chimed with a smile. Lynn quickly stepped back and circled around. When the doorman finished with Lynn's boyfriend, he waved Lynn on in, as he could tell she wasn't hiding anything. She had pulled down her shirt to reveal her cleavage before getting out of the car. They both entered the club, and took a moment to fully take in the scene.

"You see that woman next to him?"–Lynn pointed–"Go sit on the other side. You take a front row seat; I'm going to take one of the side seats," Lynn suggested, smiling.

"You sure?" her boyfriend responded, sounding surprised. He still wasn't certain this was not some kind of trick or test.

"Yeah, make the most of it," she stated, waving towards the seat. Lynn headed over to the side seat and made herself comfortable. One of the topless waitresses came and took her order while she watched her boyfriend go sit on the other side of the woman talking to Wilkinson.

She couldn't see Courtney's dad. She saw the other guy further down the bar drinking a beer.

Lynn went to look at the app again, just as the waitress returned with her cocktail. She looked up again to find her boyfriend looking back at her. Lynn was kind of surprised that he wasn't transfixed by the bare-breasted woman on the stage. *Guess not all men are alike, or guilty conscience.* she thought.

"Finally," Lynn muttered under her breath, as the GPS finally updated with the location of Courtney's dad's phone. It was only 50ft away; however, she couldn't see clearly because of the dim lighting in the club.

As a result, Lynn decided to have some fun.

"So, why you here with your friend tonight?" Chenelle inquired of Blue, who still hadn't lifted his bottle to drink, but just continued holding onto it.

"Oh, she brought me here. She said I needed to learn about women?" Blue answered, sounding a bit perplexed.

"Hey, honey, enjoying the show?" Lynn came up behind her boyfriend and placed her hand on his back.

Blue's head snapped upright at the sound of Lynn's voice, not believing it was really her.

"So, what have you learned about us women so far?" Lynn asked Wilkinson, as she sat down next to her boyfriend with her drink.

"Good question," Chenelle agreed with Lynn. "You know her?" she suggested, seeing the expression on his face.

"I erm…" Wilkinson had trouble finding the right words.

"Hey, I'm trying to enjoy the show. If you guys want to chatter, go somewhere else, and dude, stop hogging the woman. We wouldn't mind some of the one-on-one attention," the guy at the end of the bar shouted toward their group, saving Wilkinson from having to answer.

Chenelle bolted when she noticed one of the men wearing suits watching her, presumably her boss.

"It's okay. We will keep you company."–Lynn winked at Wilkinson from behind her boyfriend's back, while also flipping off the other guy–"Hey, dude, why don't you go get your dick wet somewhere else? Huh?"

He just ignored her, while Lynn could've sworn the girl on stage gave her a wink.

"Hey, my man needs some attention," she announced, as she tossed $5 onto the stage. "Enjoy," she whispered in her boyfriend's ear before trailing back to her seat, sensing Wilkinson was watching her go.

Back stage in the changing room, the door opened as Chenelle returned.

"Sorry, honey, I stayed long as I could before the boss put eyes on me. Jeanette, your customer is getting restless." Chenelle walked over to her locker.

"It's okay, Chenelle," Jeanette responded, as Sarah stood up from her seat.

"It's okay, I need to work anyway," Sarah added. She had changed into a spare costume Jeanette lent her and placed a half facial mask over her eyes.

"Oh, there is a woman out there with her boyfriend. She seems to know your friend," Chenelle noted, as Sarah and Jeanette were about to leave the changing room.

"Where she sitting?" Sarah inquired.

"At the back towards the exit, seat 12. Jeanette knows the seat orders; she'll show you," Chenelle replied. Sarah quickly ran over to her.

"Here take this," she instructed, as she passed a Franklin to Chenelle. "In about 40 minutes, take my friend into a private room. Dance for him or something; just keep him in the room."

"What you up to?" Chenelle asked.

"To stop a bad person, and what we women do best, protecting our man." Sarah winked.

"That we do," Chenelle responded, with a smile.

Sarah darted out of the changing room, and stopped at the exit onto the main floor. She saw Blue, still sitting at the bar, holding his beer.

"Good boy," she murmured, upon noticing his beer still appeared full.

She returned her focus to Jeanette, who had changed into a different outfit. She had told Sarah that she knew this guy loved the naughty nurse outfit with tight fitting panties, which didn't leave much to the imagination.

"Hey, I'm really hot for you right now. You ready for your dance?" Jeanette announced to the guy, in a very flirty tone. When he turned to face her, she immediately straddled his lap, and started to grind up and down on him. "Maybe I'll give you my number, if you are a good boy," she remarked flirtatiously. She knew the routine to get him revved up enough.

"Will you do oral too?" he questioned. The other guys in the club were extremely envious, seeing her grind up on him.

"If you pay enough, maybe."–Jeanette stood up–"Just one thing, I have a surprise for you. I may have a friend to join with me for our dance." She turned and headed off to one of the private rooms. She didn't have to look to know he was following her. The sound of his chair being knocked over crashed through the room, as he stumbled after her. He was already on his 6th beer.

She waved a finger at Sarah. This was her cue, and she entered the main room to follow after them. Blue saw her come out, and all he could do was stare, as he watched her come and go. He was completely taken aback. *I have to get to know her better.*

Lynn saw the masked woman make an entrance, and noticed every man's eyes follow her through the room. *Yes, there's Courtney's dad.* She used her phone to take a picture of him while she could in this opportune moment. He was sitting at one of the other side tables.

She got up, made sure her boyfriend was focused on the woman on stage, then made her way across the club to the other side. She turned her back before he saw her face, letting him only see her back… and her nice firm ass.

"Come with me. I'll give you a free session. I'll let you touch," she persuaded with a flirtatious tone. She quickly squatted down onto his lap, bounced back up, and headed off in the direction of the private rooms.

Lynn knew exactly how to punish him. She was reminded of Mrs. Hemlock; however, Lynn was determined to have her 'cock' and eat it too. She smirked as she headed toward a private room.

She looked over to Wilkinson and winked at him, as he watched her walk away too. Wilkinson felt his phone vibrate. When he retrieved it, he saw a text from a blocked number.

I hope you're paying attention in class.

13 CHAPTER THIRTEEN

Chris rolled over onto his side next to Raven. After their vigorous workout, sweat was still running down his forehead. Raven sat up briefly to fetch the bed cover and laid back with Chris' welcoming left arm around her shoulders. He laid on his back while Raven's head rested on his shoulder.

"This is good for you. You're starting to get biceps," Raven noted, smiling as she squeezed Chris' right arm.

They were in Raven's new room at her father's new place. It had been almost two weeks since he sent the message to Lynn, but right now, that was the farthest thing from his mind.

"I've missed you," Chris divulged, as he kissed her forehead.

"I can tell," Raven replied, looking up at him with a smile.

"So how you going to decorate your room?" Chris wondered. Currently, Raven's room had bare walls, freshly painted with some sort of neutral brown color. Her bed was situated in a corner with the left side of the bed pressed against the wall and the head of the bed just underneath the window.

Measuring 10' x 14', this room was much bigger than her old room at her mother's house. The door leading into the room was directly opposite from her closet. The bedroom on the other side of the wall belonged to her father and his new woman friend.

In an attempt to make Raven happy, her dad had told her she could invite Chris over whenever she wanted. The only problem was that it was not as easy for him to get there than when she lived at her old place. The only way Chris could get to her now was by getting someone to give him a lift to Watford, which was twenty minutes away from where he lived.

"I don't know yet, but he said I could do what I wanted with it to make it my own," Raven replied flatly.

"You okay?" Chris asked gently.

"Did I show you my collection of special stuff? It is where I keep things that mean a lot to me, like your letters to me," Raven deflected.

"Yes, you did, but you can show me again. I like seeing it," he responded, noticing how she avoided his question. Raven sat up and reached over Chris, which he didn't mind at all, as she was still topless. She retrieved a shoebox that Chris recognized, and Raven laid back down. She set the box down on his chest and he held it there with his spare hand.

Inside were all sorts of items: a Valentine card Chris had given her, the cassette tape he made for her, and the couple of letters he had written to her. He knew he wasn't that good of a writer, which was why he tried to do something different by making that tape for her.

"I love you," Chris expressed, as Raven removed the lid from the box.

"I know. The evidence is right here."–she picked up a photo of her and one of her ex-boyfriends–"I hope you don't mind me having this. I have a lot of fond memories. I will still keep this stuff even if I break up with you."

"I hope not. I want to be with you forever," he replied, sounding worried.

"I know. Me too. I'm just saying I am never going to forget the good times we make," she defended herself.

"Are you happy here?" Chris wondered.

"Least he didn't take my sisters; my mom still get to be with them." Raven returned the lid to her shoebox, and took it from Chris' chest. Then she got out of bed, placed the box under the bed, and walked over to her suitcase, which still held most of her clothes. She started to get dressed.

"Get dressed. We can head into town, show you around here," she instructed.

Chris sat up and put his shirt back on over his head.

"He is going to be back soon, isn't he?"

"Yep," she replied quickly.

"I wish I could help you. You shouldn't have to sacrifice yourself. I..." he began, but Raven cut him off. She walked back across the room.

"I told you, I don't want your help. If it wasn't me, it would be all of us. Better it is just me and he doesn't hurt them too." She picked up one of her signature hats, a small bowler hat, and paired it with her dark frame glasses.

"Where is your black stuff?" Chris questioned, with a hint of surprise in his voice. He knew Raven normally liked the shade black and preferred to wear black t-shirts and anything else black.

"Dad's new girlfriend doesn't want me to wear any black. She says it is not a nice color, like it's demonic. So, because she doesn't like it, he doesn't like it," she explained. "You ready?"

"Raven, I promise you. If there is a way to get you out of this, I am going to do it." He stood up and hugged her tight; although, she seemed a bit reluctant to hug back.

"There isn't any way, and I told you, I don't want your help. Get it?" she responded forcefully, firmly stating her point. Chris finished getting his jacket on, picked up his phone, and started to follow her.

"Okay, I got it," he sighed.

Later that night around 10pm, after he got back home from spending the day with Raven, he was on his computer somewhat distractedly playing his favorite MMO. He hated feeling powerless to do anything. He knew Raven was anything but happy, and there was something going on with her father that she wasn't telling him. He loved her. He knew that much, but she told him she didn't want his help. He was torn.

It was not long before he had played through the night into the early hours of the morning. Time usually escaped him when he entered the MMO world, allowing him to escape from reality for a bit. In the middle of a fight, a notification from Facebook popped up, causing his screen to switch to desktop from full screen. However, all Chris heard was the sound of his human mage dying to a horde of angry orcs.

"Who is Courtney?" Chris muttered aloud to himself. He clicked on the link and opened the message to read it.

He clicked over to Lynn's page and checked her friends list to find Courtney was indeed on Lynn's friends list. He checked the IP address from the source code of Courtney's message, and found the first two octets were similar to Lynn's from when she messaged him. He knew it wouldn't be a perfect match, but since the IP tracker showed Courtney's IP was in the same radius as Lynn, he felt slightly more confident.

Still, he chose to air on the side of caution and opened a message window to Lynn.

Hey, your friend Courtney is messaging me. Did you tell her to talk to me? He hit send.

He didn't have to wait long for a reply, but it was from Courtney. It appeared that she just copied the message he had sent to Lynn and sent it back to him from Courtney.

Does this prove to you Lynn is talking to me and she wants me to talk to you?

Chris accepted the invite to chat. *No, it doesn't. You could be logged into her account without her knowing about it.* He hit send.

You're smart! I like that. What you need help with? Courtney replied quickly.

Knowing he might make Raven mad, he decided to explain the situation. It was clear to him something was going on, and he wouldn't be much of a boyfriend if he didn't protect his girl.

Well, if she told you she doesn't want your help, perhaps you should listen? Courtney's response appeared on the screen.

I can't leave it alone. I know something is going on; I just don't know what. She is afraid her dad would hurt her sisters, so I believe whatever she is afraid of him doing to them, he is already doing to her. Chris sent his next message.

You saying she purposely put herself in a position to be hurt? Sounds like a big sister, which she is. Courtney's reply appeared, and the symbol flashed to signal she was typing again. *So, what do you want Lynn to do?*

Lynn is my friend and I know her reputation. I want to help stop her Raven's father from hurting anyone again. He hit send.

This time he didn't get an instant reply. Time kept ticking by, making Chris think perhaps she had left or just wanted to stop talking to him. It was approaching eight in the morning and he hadn't been to bed yet. He was about to shut down the computer to head to bed, but suddenly he heard the chime that another message had arrived.

Okay, I've relayed the information to Lynn. If she agrees to help, we will have someone come talk to you about the details in person. Do not use Facebook to message us anymore... for now. As soon as the message came in, the green light by Courtney's name disappeared, indicating she had gotten offline.

Chris had mixed feelings about what he had just done. Still, the bottom line was Raven had inspired him and he had sworn to her what he would do. He would sacrifice anything to make sure she was happy and safe, even if that meant making her mad at him and even if that meant making her break up with him. As long as she was safe, that was all that mattered to him.

He knew Raven was brave and strong. She had proven that by putting herself on the knife's edge with her father, instead of her sisters. She had proven her strength in countless other ways too, and yet, Chris still had an uneasy sense he had done right by seeking Lynn's assistance.

14 CHAPTER FOURTEEN

Courtney's dad entered the private room. The lights were dimmed to a low red glow. The song "Lick" by Joi started playing. He sat down when he watched the girl enter. She wasn't dressed like the other women in the club.

Lynn kept her back to him as she started to pulsate her hips in a slow circular motion to start off the lap dance. He held her hips while she gradually stepped backwards and bent over to display her ass before him. He started to rub her ass. Then she sat down on his lap and began to grind back and forth. She could feel him start getting excited.

"So, what brings you here tonight?" she questioned, while making sure to still keep her back to him.

"I am here to meet some people," he replied, as he started to focus on her body.

"Good boy," Lynn commented in flirty tone. She unbuttoned her pants and let them drop to the floor, revealing her red G-string. She stood back up, took a step forward, and bent over, very clearly showing off her ass.

"What are you meeting them for?" Lynn inquired.

"I can't tell you," he answered.

"Aww, but it's hot in here. I really want to take my shirt off for you." Lynn turned to the side and gave him a quick wink, as she lifted her t-shirt showing a glimpse of the side of her breast still covered by her bra.

Excitement getting the better of him, "I'm here to give something to these people," he remarked, his excitement suddenly getting the better of him. He started to lay back and began to slowly rub himself from the outside of his pants. "Take it off... Please..." he begged.

Lynn started to rub her hands over her bare ass, and her breasts, which were still covered by her shirt.

"That bulge looks uncomfortable. Why not take your pants off? Then maybe I'll feel like taking my shirt off," Lynn teased further, as she allowed him to see her hand slowly slide down the front of her G-string.

He quickly unfastened his pants and pushed them down to his ankles.

"Boxers too," Lynn coaxed, as she slowly started to lift her shirt up and over her head. He did as ordered, revealing his firm erection.

"You ready for your reward, big boy? If so, close your eyes and lean back."

She let him watch her undo the clasp on her bra before he did as ordered.

"Okay, my eyes are closed. I'm ready," he affirmed.

With her bra still on, Lynn turned around to face him, and the next thing he heard was the sound of a camera taking a picture.

"What?" he suddenly asked, sounding alarmed. He opened his eyes to see the girl in front of him. "You're..."

Lynn put her finger in front of her mouth, signaling him to be quiet. She stepped forward and squatted down in front of him.

"Say anything, the picture goes straight to your wife and Courtney. They being saved remotely, not just on my phone."

She started to stroke him to keep him excited. Then she placed her mouth over his firm length, taking it all into her mouth. She took a selfie with him still in her mouth. She began to stand back up, removing him from her mouth, but continued to stroke it his erection.

"You're a bad man, taking advantage of your daughter's friend. I think it will ruin you if they ever found out you cheated on your wife."

"What do you want?" he pleaded, realizing he was stuck between feeling pleasured and being caught in an extremely compromising position.

"You are going to leave here after this and go home. Delete that recording of your interrogation. If the police get that recording from you, your life will be over," she threatened.

"It's okay, I'm not going to leave you hanging like this." She jolted his erection to get her point across.

She stood up and straddled his lap. After moving her G-string to the side, placed him inside her, and started to move up and down along his length. Again, she put her arm out to the side to take pictures of the two of them, including a close-up of him inside her.

"I know you're enjoying this, but I'm very expensive compared to the other girls here. Open your phone and transfer $20,000 to this account here." She held her phone in front of him to display the account number.

She kept going until she felt herself climax, then got off.

"No wonder your wife is bored with you. You're not very good, are you? Perhaps it was the stress. Who knows?" She got up and redressed herself.

"If the money is not confirmed in an hour, they get everything," she threatened again. She reached into his pants pocket, pulled out his wallet and took $40 out.

"For the dance," she commented, with a wink.

She turned and opened the curtain. Before stepping outside, she turned to face him.

"Hey, don't be so blue. You got your dick wet, right?" As she stepped out of the room, she noticed the woman with the half mask standing by the entrance to one of the other private rooms. Sarah turned and saw Lynn. She didn't smile, Lynn winked at her before walking back to the main bar area.
Sarah put her ear to the curtain of the room where Jeanette had taken her *client*. Judging from the sounds, Jeanette was still keeping him busy with her dancing.

Sarah decided she had to know what Lynn was up to, though she had a feeling she knew what it was. Sarah made her way to the room just in time to see the man she and Blue were supposed to be meeting.

"You didn't…" Sarah remarked, sounding disappointed. "Tell me you didn't just do something stupid with her." The man looked up with a guilty expression on his face.

"Who are you?" he questioned.

She removed her mask.

"Oh," he mustered.

"You still have the recording?" Sarah inquired.

"I can't give it to you. She said she would tell my family if she finds out I gave it to you," he pleaded.

Sarah was beyond furious. She marched over, forced him down into a chair, and placed one of her 4" high heels directly on top of his groin.

"Give me your phone. If you didn't think with this,"–she pressed down on him and twisted her foot a little–"then you wouldn't be in this position."

She held out her right hand in front of him, palm facing up. He reluctantly gave her his phone.

"How did she know you were here?" Sarah demanded.

"I don't know," he answered. Sarah pressed down on his groin again, causing him to scream out in pain.

"I don't know, I swear!" he exclaimed again, almost in tears.

She released his groin, but grabbed him by his shirt and pulled his face up close to hers.

"You are a cheating bastard. Get out of here. Go home and get a shower. You smell like her! Don't tell you wife where you were; you were at the station helping us with our inquiries. Don't say anything to anyone and they should be left unaware. What else did she want?" Sarah demanded.

"Money," he stated simply. "I already transferred it."

"With this?"–she raised the phone and received a nod in response–"Get out of here, now! Don't say anything to anyone."

Sarah let go of him and stormed out of the room. She was still wearing the skimpy outfit Jeanette had lent her. It didn't exactly provide any pocket space, so she did what she could and placed the phone inside her bra. She made sure to turn it off first, hoping the guy was too drunk by this point to care or notice.

Sarah return to her position outside the other private room to wait for her big entrance. Meanwhile back in the bar, Blue was enjoying the next act. He still hadn't taken a sip of his drink. He was starting to wonder where Sarah had gone. However, he was not all that concerned apparently, as the thought vanished just as fast as it came once the woman shook her chest in front of him. Then she went to place a hand on his lap.

"Keep those hands where I can see them," Chenelle instructed, standing behind him again.

He turned to see her again, and found she was wearing a new outfit from the one she'd worn on stage.

"I'm sorry for before. We can't stay hanging around too much on one person; the boss doesn't like it."

"It's okay," Blue said, smiling.

"If you're feeling the urge too hard to resist, why not come with me? I'll give you that dance I promised you," Chenelle mused.

"But I don't know where my friend is…" Blue commented.

"It's okay. We will find her," Chenelle replied, taking his hand to lead him over to a private area.

Sarah could hear two people talking, getting louder as they walked closer. She recognized Blue's voice, and chose to keep her back to them.

As Chenelle and Blue stepped into the area, Blue noticed the masked woman standing by the room with her back to him. He stood and stared at her for a moment. Chenelle didn't notice until she had arrived at the room she was going to use and held the curtain open. She turned to find him staring away from her, and followed his gaze. Seeing he was staring at Sarah's back, she smiled and walked back up to him.

"See something you like?" Chenelle suggested, as she held his hand.

"She is really beautiful," he observed, as Chenelle fell behind him to look over his shoulder at Sarah, who couldn't resist smirking.

"You think so, huh?" Chenelle commented. She winked at Sarah, who seemed to be partially looking over her shoulder.

"Yeah, she is really nice. What about my friend?" he asked.

"Thank you, Blue," Sarah muttered to herself quietly, while nodding to Chenelle to acknowledge the wink. She felt happy about the compliment. Though when she saw Chenelle close the curtain behind them as they entered a private room, she started to feel jealous that Chenelle was alone with him.

"So, it's time we talked." Sarah overheard Jeanette's voice from inside the room. That was her cue. She entered the room to see Jeanette was completely topless and wearing just her panties. The very drunk man now was completely relaxed and limp in the chair.

"He is my friend, as I promised," Jeanette stated. "Just follow my lead," she whispered to Sarah, as they started to dance erotically.

"Hey there," Sarah mused seductively. The guy just raised his beer as acknowledgment.

"He doesn't look like a real man, Jeanette," Sarah observed, starting a conversation with Jeanette.

"No, I is man," he interjected. He was so drunk, he was slurring his words. Jeanette started to rub her ass in Sarah's groin while she leaned forward, blew him an air kiss, and pressing her chest up toward him.

"You sure? You don't seem to be able stay hard for Jeanette here?" Sarah reached around to Jeanette's groin, and used her palm on the outside of Jeanette's panties to rub her down below. Jeanette stood back up and turned around. She moved within inches of Sarah's face, as if they were about to kiss, but froze and went down to start kissing Sarah's chest.

"I fuck you both good. I am man," he declared.

"Uh huh, sure," Sarah retorted. "We hear that from a lot of guys, and never live up to the hype."

"I am man. I was a man before," he slurred.

"You were a man before, but not now?" Jeanette giggled.

"No, yes, I was man before. I sorted out someone," he replied.

"Who did you sort out?" Sarah asked.

"Bitch from here last time. She made fun of me; I sorted her out," he answered.

Sarah moved onto his lap and started to grind on him, as Jeanette rubbed her chest in Sarah's face.

"What do you mean?" Jeanette questioned.

"I love the girl from here. I went to see her and she was fucking another man, her husband," he explained.

"Wow, that would make me very angry," Sarah stated.

Blue started to overhear the talking from the other room through the speaker system that normally played music.

"That's my friend." He immediately stood up, and Chenelle stopped dancing for him, as they both listened.

"Yeah, I angry," the drunk man replied, still slurring his words. Sarah stood back up, turned and was kind of disappointed. He was still limp.

"So, what did you do?" Sarah wondered. She just looked at him as she stopped dancing, followed by Jeanette.

"I killed them. See? I a real man," he stated.

Hearing that, Blue stormed out of his room, went straight over to the other room and barged through the curtain. He froze for a split second upon seeing the nearly naked woman and the half-masked woman, who he now knew was his partner.

"You're under arrest for manslaughter." He retrieved his badge from his sock to display to everyone.

"You're a cop!?" Chenelle cried out, sounding alarmed.

Blushing and feeling embarrassed as he went by the naked women, he pulled out his spare cuffs and placed them on the man.

"Your boss will let us have the recording?" Sarah asked Jeanette.

"Wait! You're a cop too?" Chenelle was dumbfounded, as she glanced back and forth between Sarah and Blue's back.

Blue reached under the man's arm and picked him up, as he was clearly too drunk to stand on his own. Blue pulled him to a standing position.

"You mind?" Blue asked Jeanette, nodding to the guy's pants.

"Oh, sure." Jeanette went and pulled up the guy's pants.

"Thanks. Well, let's go. You have a cell with your name on it," Blue declared. He received a drunken ramble in reply that no one could understand.

All that time, Sarah had a proud smile across her face while watching her partner.

"Wait!" Chenelle blurted out, as both Blue and Sarah prepared to leave. "You never answered that girl's question."

"What girl?" Sarah asked,

"That girl and her boyfriend. She asked him what he had learned about women so far. He got out of answering it before because of him."–Chenelle pointed to the drunk man in handcuffs–"So what did you learn?" Chenelle repeated.

"Yes, I'd like to hear the answer to that too?" Sarah joined in. Jeanette, Chenelle, and Sarah were all looking at him.

"That I would be afraid of you all, if I made you angry and against me," Blue responded. "Why didn't you want me to drink? So I could make the arrest?" he asked Sarah. Sarah stayed silent. It was Jeanette who answered.

"She didn't want you to drink because the more you drink, the more your base desire would have come out for any woman that came in front of you. We target people that are drinking because we get paid better if you're drunk."

"Take him to the car. I'll join you once I change," Sarah instructed.

Blue did as he was told. Once he got to the main area, the bouncers instantly formed a barrier behind him to follow him out, making sure he didn't start a scene. However, as it was approaching 04:00, the crowd was slowly dissipating to head home.

On the way out, he noticed Lynn in a side seat with her boyfriend now.

"Who is that man?" Lynn's boyfriend asked her.

"Someone from back home. I'm playing a rather long game with him. You having fun?" she asked her boyfriend, while she gave Blue a wink.

"Yeah, I am having a great time now." He leaned back as Lynn held his long firm erection in her hand.

"I did tell you I would give you a hand," Lynn stated, smiling as she leaned over and kissed him.

Moments later, Lynn saw Sarah come out of the back room and walk across the floor. Quickly, Lynn got up, leaving her boyfriend stranded as he quickly did up his fly. She walked over to Sarah.

"I don't think we've met properly. I believe we have a mutual friend?" Lynn suggested warmly.

"We do," Sarah responded sharply.

"I hear you are teaching him on women. I am glad the game would get so boring if he didn't pick up his game." Lynn smiled like an innocent school girl toward Sarah.

"Is there a point to this?" Sarah questioned.

"You know, if I was playing against you, I would be more worried; however, you're on the wrong side. I mean no harm. To prove to you I am a good person, I will help out your captain and his little wife problem." Lynn kept a straight face.

"How you know about that?" Sarah's expression failed her, as surprise filled her face.

"Good night, Detective Sarah." Lynn turned and went to rejoin her boyfriend, leaving Sarah with no option but to retire from the club and join Blue.

14.2 CHAPTER FOURTEEN POINT TWO

Lynn walked into Credo's the same morning, just after dropping her boyfriend off at home and heading straight to work.

"Long night?" Lola wondered, seeing the look on Lynn's face. Black circles loomed over Lynn's eyes; she looked exhausted.

"Did he ever respond?" Lynn asked, accepting the strong black coffee Lola just fetched from their coffee machine for her.

"Yeah, he did. How close are you to him? Your puppy?" Lola questioned.

"We've had our moments. I don't think he will be a fan of White Sox anytime soon," Lynn laughed, remembering the trick she had played on Chris so long ago. "Why? What's going on?" It was getting hard for Lynn to think and do simple things the longer she tried, though the coffee was helping her wake up.

"It appears to me that his friend is a lot like you. His friend is in trouble," Lola tactfully stated.

"His girlfriend!" Lynn corrected her.

"Indeed," Lola acknowledged the remark. "Well, he doesn't know what to do. His *girlfriend*, he feels, is getting hurt by her father. She is sacrificing her happiness to protect her sisters. He wants to do something, but she has told him she didn't want his help."

"Which means she wants his help, she just won't admit it," Lynn sighed.

"Well, I know now what cards I've been dealt."

"What did the flop tell you?" Lola asked.

"That someone needs to be punished and dealt with, that I can get my friend out of the way for a while, that I can get someone on the turn," Lynn explained, with a sneaky smile.

"So, what's your plan?" Lola pushed.

"Where is Courtney?" Lynn responded. "I want you to transform her to look like me as much as you can. We, or more actually Courtney, will help go help Chris," Lynn explained. "Except we are going to make my friend think Courtney is me and have him follow her."

"So, you're going to bluff him." Courtney interjected, as she appeared at the door of the back room. "Sorry, I guess I fell asleep. How did I get here?"

"I brought you here in the car. You were out! You want a coffee?" Lola smiled.

"It's okay, you fell asleep while we waited for the puppy to respond. He didn't start talking for a while, until you were already sleeping," Lynn explained.

"What happened to you? You look flushed; your cheeks are glowing," Courtney noticed, pointing towards Lynn.

"We had a long night. We going to help out the puppy," Lynn deflected.

"No, it's more than that. You're still wearing the same clothes. You would have changed, knowing you."–Courtney snapped her fingers–"You got laid! You jumped his bones finally, didn't you?" Courtney started smiling, while Lola immediately spun around on the spot.

"No, it isn't that," Lynn lied, giggling and blushing.

"Oh, come on. It is all over your face. Come on! Tell us girls what happened! How was it? Is he well stacked?" Courtney giggled.

Lynn turned to look directly at Lola. It was a clear expression of *save me*.

"Hey, Courtney, Lynn has paid for you to have a makeover. We should get started before we have to open. Lynn, you go sleep. You're no good to me as you are now," Lola ordered, picking up on Lynn's hint.

"Alright. Oh hey, when is the next time Mrs. Hemlock is in again?" Lynn wondered.

"Hey, don't think I'll forget about it," Courtney quipped.

"Mrs. Hemlock is down for this coming Friday. Why?" Lola asked.

"I have a promise to keep. Night," Lynn said, as she headed into the backroom to sleep.

"Hey!" Lola remarked, stepping up close behind Lynn. "Who was it?" Lola nudged.

Lynn glanced around to make sure Courtney was out of earshot, as she raised her phone and showed Lola the first picture she took of Courtney's dad.

"Clever girl, but get a better poker face... and fast," Lola commented, as she turned and walked away.

978-0692579237 (C B Bartram Books)

16 CHAPTER SIXTEEN

"Well, this is going to be good," Captain Howard explained, as he shut the door to his office behind Detective Sarah and Sergeant Wilkinson. "Care to explain why the US taxpayer is going to be paying for you to see strippers?"

"Dancers," Sarah corrected.

"Alright! *Dancers*," the Captain corrected himself.

"We were working my case as ordered, Cap," Sarah explained.

"And it just so happened the perp for your murder was there?" Howard questioned. "At the same time and place where the person I ordered you to stay away from also was there?"

"He was?" Wilkinson turned to Sarah in surprise.

"And…" the Captain continued over Wilkinson, "I suppose you didn't know his perp would be there too?"

"As in our report, Captain, following up a lead I received, I got reliable information my perp would be there last night. The vic was a dancer at the club and I knew the club would be eager to help with bringing him to justice. It was Wilkinson's cool head not getting carried away that allowed him to make the arrest," Sarah explained. "His first official recorded arrest since being here, Captain," she added, smiling.

"Did they know you were detectives? Last thing we need is the perp filing an entrapment case against us?"

"The door-persons were unaware except for our agent working undercover. She gave me the code clearance that we were good, and their management knew and were okay with us with the sting."

"Agent?" Wilkinson asked, somewhat stunned. A knock sounded on Howard's office door and one of the female patrol officers from downstairs entered. Her hair was done up into a bun as she walked into the Captain's office.

"Here is my report you asked for, sir."–she handed over a file, and winked at Wilkinson as she turned around–"Hope you had good time... erm." With a beaming smile across her face, she left and closed the door behind her. Wilkinson sat there stunned, while Sarah was having an incredibly hard time trying to resist laughing.

"She is very talented. Isn't she, Wilkinson?" Howard asked, to break the silence, while smiling wide. "It's okay, you're not the first. You will not be the last," he sighed. "Well, I'll let this drop, as I don't want to spoil your first arrest." Howard reached down to his right side. The last time he did this, he had pulled out Wilkinson's gun back on his first day.

"Your reward, Detective."–he placed a bottle of scotch on the desk and pushed it towards Wilkinson. "I would share this with your partner here. She tells me you can hold your liquor."–he winked–"Alright, go on." Wilkinson got up to leave.

"I'll join you in a moment," Sarah stated, smiling at him. She waited for him to close the door as he left.

"What is it? You haven't spoken to me alone like this unless you had to," the Captain remarked, as he leaned back in his seat.

"Cap, did you tell anyone about your wife?" Sarah asked directly.

"What is this about exactly, Detective?" Howard turned this into a more serious affair by using her title.

"Sir, forgive me, I need to know," she insisted.

"Well, my attorney, her attorney, her boyfriend, everyone in the department knows. That is it. Now tell me what this is about?" he obliged her request.

Sarah looked back at the door to make sure Blue was actually gone before answering.

"Cap, before I left the club after the arrest, Lynn, his perp, approached me. She told me she would prove she is a good person by helping you with your little wife problem. She also told me I was on the wrong side."

She stood in silence, allowing her Captain to fully digest the information she had just given him. He stood and stepped over to look out the window.

"Do you feel like helping her?" he asked, while still staring out the window. "I mean, don't women stick together?"

"No, Cap, on both accounts," she answered sternly.

"Alright, thank you for telling me. You can go," he muttered quietly, staring out the window.

"Cap?" she attempted to ask, trying to push the ignored issue.

"Just go, Detective. Thank you." He waited and kept staring out the window until he heard the door close before returning to his desk. He pulled open the upper left drawer of his desk, which held a picture of him and a woman on their wedding day. A gold wedding band laid discarded atop the photo.

Seeing Sarah come out of the office, Wilkinson walked over to her.

"So, what now?" he wondered.

Sarah distractedly looked back towards the filtered glass of Howard's office door.

"Hmm?"–she paused–"Oh. Nothing much we can do, we have more cases to do."

"What about Lynn? She was taunting us last night. And did I pass my training on women?" he questioned.

"Come on, let's go." She walked past him to head down to the police station's underground parking garage for their cars.

Wilkinson followed behind her quickly. While they were waiting for the elevator doors to open, Sarah turned on the spot and kissed him fully on the mouth. As the doors opened, she instantly broke it off and stepped straight into the elevator, followed by Wilkinson. Despite feeling surprised and confused, he had to make an effort to remain silent while the other people exited the elevator.

"Please don't keep me wondering. Tell me, what that was for?" he inquired, with a shocked tone in his voice.

"You did really well last night. You could have followed Chenelle into the room without a second thought, but you were concerned about me, and your honesty. I heard you saying I was beautiful. As I said before, you are sweet. Most men would have lost their heads and followed their dicks, like our informant friend." She punched the wall, as she relived the night through her memories.

"What happened with that?" Wilkinson asked.

"You did not under sell your perp at all. You know she was there last night, right?" Sarah questioned. She received a nod in response.

"Well, she happened. Blacked mailed our informant. He wouldn't have been in a position to be blackmailed, if he didn't allow his dick to lead him."—she sighed—"You get where I am going with this, right?"

Wilkinson just stared at her blankly.

"She had sex with him," Sarah stated flatly.

"Bloody hell, really?" Wilkinson exclaimed.

"I think that is the most British thing I've heard you say," she replied, laughing. "But it is not all bad… I got his phone and the recording, also one of her account numbers. She made him pay her off."

"So, we have leads now to follow." He became very excited hearing this new development in the case.

"Yes, but now we have to wait, not overplay our hand."—she pulled her car keys out of her pocket and turned to face him—"We are going over to my place. Going to cook you dinner. I bet you haven't had a home cooked meal since you got here," she suggested.

"I think I just figured out something about women, and why you kissed me on my cheek before and kept me guessing," Wilkinson declared, as he suddenly had an epiphany.

"Oh? Do tell," Sarah replied, with a smile across her face.

"You wanted me to keep thinking about you. Keeping me guessing about why you kissed me actually keeps me thinking about you. It appears how women operate, they use their minds to be manipulative, while men are more physical than mental," he explained.

"Try not to stereotype, Blue; there is exceptions on both sides. Sadly, blonde women got the stereotype of dumb blonde-haired person for a reason. However, in turn, to reinforce my point, not all blonde haired women are dumb," Sarah pointed out.

"Oh," he said sadly.

"What's wrong? Why so sad?" she asked, seeing the sudden change in his mood. Wilkinson handed the bottle of scotch to Sarah. "What? Why?"

"It was your arrest, not mine. You had the entire thing setup, which means I didn't do anything. I was your proxy," he sighed.

"No, Blue," Sarah attempted to reassure him. "It was your arrest. I told you I was going to help you pop your cherry, but it was all you in the club. I had no control whether you drank your beer or not. I did not know if you would get lost with the naked women in front of you. It was your arrest," she insisted.

"It was our arrest; I couldn't have done it without you," Wilkinson responded, as they got into the car to start the journey to her home.

"I know," she stated with a smirk, as she revved up the engine and pulled out onto the streets.

"So… who was your favorite?" Sarah wondered.

"Nice try. I'm not falling for that trap," Wilkinson answered, sensing the test.

"No, seriously, it's okay. I just like to know who you liked. You seemed to get on well with Chenelle," she pushed.

"You know who my favorite was." He took a deep breath.

"Right, Chenelle," she answered for him, pushing his buttons.

"No! The woman with tattoos on her body. The one that had the people staring at her as she came out of the room. The one I saw in the private area... You!" he finally admitted.

"You're really sweet, Blue, or you are learning fast, but either way you never see me like that again. Okay?" She turned quickly, prompting Blue for an answer.

"Okay?" she urged. "It was part of the job. You understand?"

Wilkinson looked down toward his feet.

"If I had known that would have been the last time, I would have got a picture to save the moment."

"You mean to jack off to? Sorry, Blue. You have to rely on good old fashion memory."

It was a forty-minute drive over to Sarah's place. Sarah got Blue a drink and retreated to the kitchen to start making dinner.

"Why do you keep looking at Facebook?" Sarah shouted from the kitchen.

"Oh, her Facebook account was active last night. I was seeing if she is still on," Blue replied.

"You know there is groups for Facebook stalkers. You need a twelve step program," she chuckled. "I'm making roasted turkey with turkey gravy and mashed potatoes. You can pour the wine. I have red and white; pick whatever you like," Sarah announced.

Sarah's apartment was corner condo on West 57th Street, with a wide open floor plan. There were several huge windows to allow light to flood inside. A white three seat couch was situated at one end, surrounded by four loveseats. A glass coffee table with a black metal frame sat in the middle of the couches on top of a beige rug. A few feet away from the main seating area was a circular dining table. The kitchen would have normally been open as well, but Sarah had installed a privacy wall to separate the spaces.

Wilkinson walked over to the wine rack on the wall, which displayed a large variety of wine bottles. Underneath, there were a series of decorative wine barrels displayed. Wilkinson started to peruse the selection.

"You said turkey, right?" he hollered toward the kitchen.

"Yep!" Sarah answered almost immediately. Wilkinson saw Pinot Noirs, Zinfandel red wines, and a couple of fancy champagne bottles. Then he came across a bottle perfectly suited for their meal, a Sauvignon Blanc, a fine white wine. He picked up a couple of wine glasses and walked into the kitchen.

"You in the middle of something difficult or do you have a moment?" he asked, displaying the bottle.

"Erm…"–Sarah glanced around quickly–"Yeah, everything is safe for a moment. Why? Hmm, good choice," she declared, as she noticed the bottle.

"It's customary as chef and hostess, you get the first glass of wine. It's good luck," Wilkinson remarked, as he uncorked the bottle and poured Sarah a very generous portion into her glass.

"Are you trying to get me sloshed, good sir?" Sarah asked in a mock English accent, as she accepted the glass. "Cheers!" She raised her glass to Wilkinson, as they both took a sip.

Sarah finishing cooking their meal. They both sat down and enjoyed the meal. Sarah's hunch had been right, Wilkinson gobbled up his food.

"Nothing like home-cooked food." He sat back in his seat to relax, rubbing his full stomach as he drank more wine.

Suddenly, the door buzzer sounded.

"Who is that?" Wilkinson questioned.

"Your reward." Sarah winked as she got up and just pressed the buzzer to unlock the main building entrance. "Go have a seat on the couch," Sarah instructed, with a large smile beaming at Blue. He did as requested when they heard a knock on the door.

"What is going on?" Wilkinson prodded. Sarah unlocked the door and opened it to allow the visitor inside.

"It was your first time at a club and you didn't get to enjoy…"

"Hey there," Chenelle interrupted Sarah.

"I wanted our private dance," Sarah said smiling. She took Chenelle's coat to hang it up for her.

"Our dance got interrupted before, and I did promise you a dance!" Chenelle declared.

Sarah ran across the room, moved the coffee table out of the way, and sat next to Blue, ready to enjoy the show.

"Here is your glass."–Sarah passed him his wine glass–"If you're holding your glass, we will know where your hands are," Sarah giggled.

Chenelle put a small MP3 player down on the table to start her music playlist. It began with a slow song, *Cold* by Annie Lennox. She started to dance erotically, much more than Blue had seen her do on stage.

Blue kept looking back and forth between Sarah and Chenelle, not sure where to keep his gaze. Chenelle tore off her shirt to reveal her lace bra. She got up close and personal to Sarah, and leant forward pushing her chest into Sarah's face. Sarah grabbed onto Blue's knee, as she was apparently finding it difficult to resist touching. Chenelle stood up, turned around, squatted down with her ass between Sarah's legs, and began rubbing up against her groin.

Sarah's hand suddenly leapt from Blue's knee to his groin, and she began stroking him through his pants. Apparently what Chenelle was doing started to feel overwhelmingly good. When Chenelle stood up, she turned and offered her hand to Sarah. Upon accepting, Chenelle pulled her up from the couch, and they started to dance very slowly and very erotically.

Wilkinson had been left helpless, as he watched Chenelle slowly start to unfasten Sarah's pants. Chenelle pulled the top part of Sarah's pants apart and slid her hand down Sarah's panties, as she danced around behind Sarah and started to kiss softly and blow gently onto the side of her neck.

Sarah took a quick glance at Blue, seeing the dumb look on his face.

"Enjoying the show?" she asked him, as she let out a moan when Chenelle started to touch again.

"I knew you be great to dance with," Chenelle giggled.

Sarah broke away from Chenelle, turned around to face her.

"Shall we?" Sarah suggested, as she broke away from Chenelle and turned around to face her. She glanced sideways at Blue to get her point across. "I don't think it is right he gets to keep his clothes on."

"I agree!" Chenelle exclaimed, before Blue could fully make sense of what was happening. Sarah grabbed the wine glass from him and threw it across the room, smashing it. She grabbed him by his shirt and pulled him up from the couch.

"You know what I said before?" Sarah asked Blue, as Chenelle started to rub his groin.

"Yes?" Blue replied nervously.

"I lied," Sarah stated simply, as she tore his shirt open to reveal his firm chest. "Your innocence, it's kind of a turn on. I want to corrupt you." Sarah and Chenelle pulled him into the bedroom. Blue's cellphone dropped to the floor, displaying Lynn's Facebook page, but it laid there forgotten, as he was about to get an experience of a life time.

17 CHAPTER SEVENTEEN

"It's time to play my hand," Lynn said to herself. She had just woken up after her nap in the backroom. She found a change of clothes to borrow and quickly redressed. She looked at her reflection in the mirror and slapped herself.

"Never do that again," she reprimanded herself. "Clearly when you're tired, you are a very easy read."

She took a deep breath in, and as she exhaled, she opened the door and stepped out onto the shop floor of Credo's.

Lola had her back to the door, as she was still working on Courtney. Lynn walked over to the coffee machine and looked at the clock; it was almost nine. The sound of the coffee machine made Courtney look over in that direction.

"Oh, hey," Courtney announced. "Thank you for my makeover."

"You're welcome. You're a good friend. You deserve to be treated," Lynn replied, as she started to drink her coffee. "So, Courtney, how you feel about taking a trip? I want to help Chris, but I can't return. Immigration rules, you see. So, you are my only hope of getting help to Chris."

"What is going on with that? Fill me in. What does he need help with?" Courtney asked excitedly.

"His girlfriend, Raven, is in trouble. She is being all noble and doesn't want Chris to help, so Lynn is going to help. She technically didn't tell him that she didn't want help from anyone," Lola explained.

"After you are done here, I will take you to your house, so you can get packed, and I'll explain it to your dad. You should not have any problems from them. That is, if you want to go?"

"Of course, I said, or more accurately, I promised to help you, plus it be exciting to see another country," Courtney stated.

"So, I take it you will not be working today?" Lola asked, already knowing the answer.

"I'll be working, just not here," Lynn responded.

"Tomorrow, make sure Sharon uses this station please," Lynn instructed, as she walked over to the same station she had used to wash Sharon's, Mrs. Hemlock's, hair.

"Why?" Lola wondered.

"It is her lucky seat," Lynn lied.

"Lynn!" Lola saw straight through Lynn's response. Lynn was kind of stuck on how to put this in a way that Lola would understand and Courtney would not. She clicked her fingers as it came to her.

"It will be my river card, after the turn."

"Hmm, I see," Lola replied, understanding Lynn's cryptic message.

"Well, I don't," Courtney interjected, sounding confused.

Lynn reached up and placed her phone onto the top shelf, close to the edge.

"Don't worry about it, Courtney. Just enjoy your time here." She turned around and leaned against the counter to watch Courtney. "It's not often us girls get to enjoy being pampered. Lola, I'm going to use my spare phone, okay?"

Lola nodded in acknowledgment, as Lynn walked over to the counter holding the cash register. She pulled open the draw to reveal about twenty different phones. She selected an iPhone 4S with a pink-colored case and she closed the drawer.

"Do you have a passport, Courtney?" Lynn questioned.

"I do. Mom has it," she answered.

"There, done! You look gorgeous if I do say so myself," Lola exclaimed. She stood up, removed Courtney's apron, and swept away any loose strands of hair off Courtney.

"How do I look, Lynn?" Courtney asked. She stood there with her palms open to either side of her, and she looked up and down before checking her reflection in the mirror.

"Simply stunning, take a look." Lynn gestured to the mirror.

"OMG!!!!" Courtney squealed in excitement, as she looked in the mirror. Lynn and Lola both had to cover their ears.

"You like it then?" Lola asked, laughing.

"I love it! Lynn, we're sisters now!" Courtney giggled, as she ran over to stand next to Lynn. She turned her around, so they both stood facing the mirror. Seeing the resemblance, Lynn chuckled as well.

"We look great!" Lynn exclaimed. "Well, come on. We need to get going and you need to get changed. You are going to be flying to England today!"

"Today?" Courtney asked, surprised. "How do you have money for the air fare?"

"I work here. I been saving my money, nothing special. This is important." Lynn turned to wave at Lola, and saw her mouth the words *be careful* with a worried look on her face.

The ride over to Courtney's home was uneventful. Lynn pulled up outside and parked on the street.

"Is your home electric heat?" she inquired.

"Oil," Courtney answered. "It's very expensive too." They got out of the car and went inside the house.

"You go ahead and pack. I'll talk to your parents," Lynn ordered, loud enough to get her parents' attention and announce their presence.

"Hey, Lynn, we are in here. Talk to us about what?" Courtney's mom hollered from the front room.

"I needed to talk with you, about Courtney," Lynn began, eyeing Courtney's father. "My work, Credo's, needs someone to meet one of our agents that helps us import the products we use on our customers. So, Lola, my boss, has paid for Courtney and I to fly to England to accompany her."

"Oh, I don't know about that," her mom said at first. Her husband stayed silent, looking directly at Lynn.

"Well, I have some pictures to show you if that would help," Lynn added, looking directly at Courtney's dad. He coughed.

"Erm... I don't think we can hold her back from this. It's business related and they will be accompanied by her boss, Lola. It would do her good, give her experience," her dad proposed.

"Well, if you think so. How long is the trip?" her mom asked.

"It shouldn't be too long, two weeks at most. I wanted to show her around my old place." Lynn focused on keeping a straight face while maintaining direct eye contact with Courtney's father. "We are leaving today though, soon as she is done packing."

"Oh, I see. I better go up and help her pack then." Courtney's mom quickly got up to go up to Courtney's room. Lynn could tell she was trying to hold back tears at the thought of her baby girl going away.

With Courtney's mom's departure from the room, Lynn was left with the man she'd just had sex with last night. She smiled directly at him.

"Miss me?" she commented, with a smirk. "Don't worry, you're not in trouble. This is just business." She noticed he seemed worried.

"Does she suspect you?" she questioned, thinking that was why he was worried.

"You destroyed the recording, right?" she asked next. His eyes darted around the room, searching for an exit before he answered.

"Yeah, I did. I made sure you got your money."

"Indeed," Lynn replied, not feeling convinced at all. "I'm going to go help Courtney."

Lynn started to make her way upstairs when she bumped into Michael. He was on one of his food runs to the kitchen between GTA sessions.

"Heya, Michael," she said flirtatiously, making an effort to show a little extra skin.

"Oh, hey," he responded, starting to stumble. "I'm about to take your sister to the airport. You should come with. See her off?" she suggested, while smiling and batting her eyes at him.

"How soon until you go?" he questioned.

"I'd save or close out your game now, but I wouldn't jerk it. I'd save it if I were you."—she winked—"I'll let you know. I'll call for you when we come back down."

"Alright." Michael bolted back to the basement, leaving his plate of food on the table. Lynn continued heading upstairs to Courtney's room.

When she got to the top of the stairs, she noticed what she was looking for and walked over to the wall space between the doors to Courtney's room and her parents' room. Their smart thermostat was there, connected to their local wifi.

"Guess we will see how smart it is," Lynn muttered under her breath.

It was in the middle of the summer, so they were not using their heat; however, at night, it would get cold. Checking to make sure no one was around, she pulled out her iPhone and opened up the application she knew would control this thermostat. She made sure she was connected to the home's wifi, and tested the connection to reduce the current setting to 00.

She pressed the safety lock on the app to make sure the furnace was turned off. Now, it would only be possible to turn it back on from her phone, or more accurately, her iCloud account. She shut off her phone and put it away, as she knocked on Courtney's door.

"Is it okay for me to come in?" Lynn asked through the door.
Five minutes later, which was about twenty minutes in woman's time, the door to Courtney's room finally opened. The two girls went back downstairs

to a stunned Michael, as he watched what looked like two Lynn's, followed by his tearful mother.

Courtney ran over to hug her dad. Lynn quickly squeezed Michael's hand and winked to him. Michael's face immediately turned bright red. For everyone watching, this gave them something to laugh about to lighten the mood.

It wasn't long before the three of them were at the airport. Lynn made sure she was seen by every single security camera, and she even talked to several people, asking for directions, despite already knowing the way.

"Courtney, when you get over there, you need to start using my Facebook. Make posts and updates under my name, okay? Do you need me to write down my info? I already logged into it on your phone, okay?" Lynn urged.

They had just gotten to the point where they had to separate, as Courtney was about to go through security.

"Is there a point to ask why?" Courtney inquired. Her brother stood next to them, distracted by one of the advertising screens.

"It's for your protection. I don't want them people here knowing you left and you are going to be helping my friend. You may have to get your hands dirty and it be best for you if you muddy my name, not yours," Lynn explained, with a smile.

She gave Courtney a tight hug. Then Courtney hugged her brother before she turned to walk through security.

"So now what?" Michael wondered.

"We head over to arrivals," Lynn stated, as she turned to head in that direction, forgetting all about Courtney for now.

"Who we meeting? Is this why you brought me with?" Michael questioned, as he began to follow Lynn.

"I thought you could be her tour guide, show her the city?" Lynn proposed, smiling.

"Her?" he inquired, noticing the reference Lynn had made.

"You'll see. Come on. The person we are meeting got off the plane that

Courtney is going on; I had my friend Chris put her on a plane to get her out of the way," Lynn explained.

The two of them headed to the seating area for the arrivals section of the airport. Lynn saw several people were sitting there waiting. She looked for someone who looked lost, but did not see anyone in that state. Not seeing anyone. She shouted,

"We are here for Raven from England?" Lynn announced loudly. She looked around to see if anyone responded.

"I'm Raven," a girl responded, as she walked up to Lynn. She had a case on wheels behind her and her carry-on bag on her back. "You are Lynn?" Raven asked.

"Hi, yes, welcome! I'm Lynn and this is Michael." Lynn shook hands, followed by Michael. "So, tell me, what's going on? Chris said he won me a trip to New York?" Raven asked, sounding a bit skeptical.

"Yeah, well, it's a story for another time maybe, but Michael here will look after you, give you the tour, and take you to your hotel," Lynn explained, as she slipped a small wad of money into Michael's hand.

"I'll be taking you both and dropping you off at your hotel. So, let us get going, shall we? Michael be a man, help her with the luggage," Lynn instructed, with a welcoming smile. Michael jumped to take over handling Raven's luggage as they headed out of the airport.

"Well, I'm all in now," Lynn muttered to herself.

18 CHAPTER EIGHTEEN

Wilkinson awoke in the middle of the angel sandwich; he could not help but have a beaming smile across his face and wide eyes at the two very gorgeous women who just took advantage of him, not that he minded. He stole a peek and slowly lifted the bed covers. Yep, he wasn't dreaming.

Wilkinson lifted his legs up and out from under the covers to avoid disturbing the sleeping women. He noticed the time was close to 6:30, as he rolled forward and used the mattress to push himself up onto his feet in one light and simple touch. He looked around for his briefs or pants. Suddenly, he remembered they had torn them off him, so they would not be exactly wearable for work anymore. He lifted what remained of his shirt again and smiled, recalling the events of the previous night.

He began searching for his phone, and found it was not in his destroyed pants. He walked out to the main room, and the bright light from outside abruptly hit him in the face. Wilkinson sucked it up and risked being seen by the people in the other buildings who could see into the apartment, as he had just walked into the main room completely naked. On the bright side though, he could see his phone now. It was flashing a green light indicating he had Facebook notifications!

He went straight to it forgetting all thoughts of embarrassment. He bent over to pick it up.

"You better have a good reason for taking that dick out of bed!" Sarah exclaimed as she came up behind him.

He stood back up without looking and stood silent, ignoring Sarah, as he saw the notifications were about Lynn.

"Okay, you really need that stalkers group!"–Sarah craned her neck to look over his shoulder–"What is it?" she asked, giving him the benefit of the doubt.

"Lynn's Facebook is active, and posting from England. She posted 3 hours ago that she arrived in London okay. Patryk sent photos of Lynn taken from the security footage at JFK yesterday. I need to leave and go back. My Captain will want me back to go after her," he sighed, sad about the idea of leaving right after a night like last night.

"You need to apply what you learned recently, Blue."–she held onto his hips as she stood on one leg and rubbed her left knee along Blue's right leg–"You saw how I set that little thing with the club up."

"You think she is trying to mislead me?" Blue questioned.

"I think she knows the old you, not the man that you become since you came here. She is trying to mislead you," Sarah reasoned, as she started to stroke him. "Now bring your dick back to bed, I'm not done with you yet. And turn that off; you're banned from thinking about her until later. I'll have my people watch out for her."

"Sarah?" Blue interjected.

"Yeah?" She stopped and turned to face him. Without hesitation, he grabbed Sarah by her waist, pulled her in toward him, and kissed her passionately, which she returned.

"Thank you," he said genuinely, as the two of them, both stark naked, stood embracing each other in the middle of the main room in Sarah's apartment.

"Okay… I'll go on top. You get to enjoy the view," Sarah giggled, as she led him back into the bedroom.

~

Lynn used her spare keys to unlock the door to Credo's and went inside, shutting the door behind her. It wouldn't be for another hour yet until Lola arrived.

She went to the cashier counter and pulled the drawer open, most of the phones had gone except for a couple left. Lynn selected a Samsung and placed it inside her pocket, then checked to make sure she still had her iPhone before closing the drawer.

She opened the appointment book and found that yes, Mrs. S. Hemlock's was scheduled for 10:30.

"I'd love to see her get what is coming to her," Lynn muttered to herself, as she closed the appointment book. She walked over to the station she knew Mrs. Hemlock would be using to ensure her phone was still there. She pulled a small flat screw driver from her pocket and proceeded to remove the electric cover and safety circuit, which had a kill switch should anything come in contact with water, and swapped it with a traditional circuit without a kill switch before replacing the faceplate.

Lynn finished by placing one of the curling irons on the top shelf on top of her phone and plugging it into the new outlet. Lynn then unlocked the iPhone and logged into Courtney's Facebook account. She saw that *her* profile was posting about her arrival in England, showing the location as Heathrow.

"That should get you running," Lynn stated aloud, smirking. Finally, Lynn went inside Lola's office and walked behind the desk to retrieve her pack.

She knew Lola wouldn't be exactly happy if she knew the plan involved the store. However, it couldn't be helped. Sharon Howard, as that was her real name, had to be punished. Back during the first visit, she lifted Sharon's purse, retrieved her ID from it, and had gone into the back office. Sure enough, Mr. Hemlock confirmed they were not married yet, but he had hoped to marry her.

Her true husband, Lynn had realized, was the failsafe, so if everything went totally wrong, at least she would have him to fall back on. Lynn felt annoyed with herself because she felt fooled by Sharon, as she saw the ring still on her finger, and she had believed Sharon was married to the man who accompanied her. She bluffed Lynn and Lola, though Lola had yet to be informed of this. She wanted to wait until today, so Lola could not get in the way.

She wrote on a blank paper. *Start the wash and shampoo treatment for Mrs. Hemlock and then come away from her. Come in here. I'm going to punish her for lying to us.*

She left the photo copy of Sharon's ID with the note on Lola's desk where Lola would be sure to see it when she entered the office.

She looked around one last time before stepping back out to the shop floor.

Lynn put her pack on the floor and checked its contents. She pulled out the notarized letter she had made Mr. Hemlock sign. A sum of $250,000, the money that his girlfriend, Sharon, has requested from him, would be transferred to Lynn's account once Sharon was dealt with and exposed.

She placed it back in the pack, moved her clothes to the side, and found the small 2 gallon blue kerosene container.

After making sure everything was correct, she resealed her pack and headed out. She closed and locked the door to Credo's knowing this might be the last time she would be here.

Lynn walked to the curb where her car was parked, got into the Dodge, and drove off. One block away, she stopped and placed the sealed, notarized letter into the outgoing mail box.

"Okay, Wilkinson, I bet it's your action now," Lynn remarked to herself, as she drove off to the next location.

~

Sarah arched her back, as she pushed herself up and down while continuing to ride Blue. He held his hand over her mouth to muffle her moaning. Sarah was living up to her intentions to satisfy herself.

"You know it is very selfish to hog him all to yourself," Chenelle spoke up, as she sat up and moved over to kiss Blue.

Suddenly, Sarah's phone, which was lying on the side table, started to ring. She was planning to ignore it, as she was coming close to climaxing; however, the pager laying next to Sarah's phone started buzzing too.

"Well, that killed my girl boner," Sarah sighed, getting off Blue and reaching over to pick up her pager. Seeing the message, she grabbed her phone and headed toward the bathroom.

"Keep him warm," Sarah instructed. Chenelle winked in response, as Sarah walked into the bathroom and shut the door behind her.

She double-checked the message and number on her pager before typing the number into her cell phone and dialing out.

'Hi, I got your page. What's up?" Sarah began, once the call had been answered.

"Hey, it's Patryk. I kept an eye on the phone you told me about," he stated. "We've intercepted a call and text from the person of interest you asked us to watch for. You want us to allow it through to the phone?"

"Yes, do it. Where did they originate from?" Sarah questioned.

"They both originated from a phone in the United Kingdom," Patryk reported.

"Okay, allow them through. I got it from here. Thanks, Patryk," Sarah finished, and pressed the end call button.

She's good, Sarah thought. She noticed one of her bras hanging to the side, reached over, and put it on.

She opened the door to find Blue and Chenelle still having fun.

"Blue, you need to stay here," Sarah ordered.

"Not like I can go anywhere. You destroyed my clothes," he remarked, as he sat up in the bed. "What's going on?" He saw her retrieve the phone that he knew belonged to their informant.

Sarah turned on the iPhone, and saw the missed call and text message both came in from a blocked number. Knowing the FBI had already done the trace, she didn't worry about it. She opened the text to read it.

You have one chance. Call me exactly at 10:30. I know you lied, so if you don't want your life to be destroyed, you'll do what I say.

"I know where she is going to be. You need to stay here. Understood?"–she walked up to the end of the bed, staring at Blue–"You trust me to handle this? She was trying to set you up; she isn't expecting me. She expects you to be halfway to England by now." Sarah started to get dressed quickly.

"You are welcome to stay here. You can borrow some of my clothes, if you can find anything to wear, but I don't think the underwear will suit you," Sarah chuckled, as a smirk spread across her face. "I have some pants and shirts somewhere. But no matter what, stay here. Have fun with Chenelle more, okay?"

"Don't worry, I'll keep him entertained."–Chenelle sat up, beaming–"Hey, come here."

Sarah walked around the side of the bed, and Chenelle quickly hugged and kissed her.

"Thank you for a fun night. It was fun dancing for and with you," she said sincerely, with a soft smile.

"You too. Make yourself at home." Sarah finally grabbed her car keys and headed out. Blue and Chenelle both heard the front door close behind her.

"You want to go after her, don't you?" Chenelle asked, clearly seeing the sad, worried expression on Blue's face.

"Yes, I came a long way to get her. Seems odd to just sit back," he answered truthfully.

"Well, don't just sit back. Lay back down, it's my turn to enjoy you." Chenelle pushed him back down on the bed, and straddled him, picking up where Sarah left off.

~

While driving, Lynn connected her Samsung auxiliary cable to the car's audio jack. She started to dial out on her phone.

"Hi?" Courtney's voice filled the vehicle.

"Hi, Lynn," Lynn stated, starting off the call. "How is it over there in England?"

"Oh, it's you, Courtney," Courtney giggled. "It's cold and windy, just a typical British summer."

"Any update on the family trip?" Lynn asked. She heard a heavy sigh on the other end of the line.

"Yes, not everything went to plan. Chris found out the nature of how his sister was being grounded and got carried away," Courtney explained in code. "He took it on himself to drive for the family trip, instead of letting me drive."

"Is it a bad trip?" Lynn wondered.

"It is as we feared, which is why the sisters didn't come on the trip, so they wouldn't be grounded too," Courtney continued in code, so if anyone else was listening, they wouldn't be able to understand. "Chris tied a necktie on father. Now, he is hiding. May have to bring him back home for a while for a time out," Courtney reported.

"Well, keep updated on when you are flying back," Lynn concluded, as she ended the call using the controls on the steering wheel, so she could keep both hands on the wheel.

It wasn't long before Lynn drove up to a gas station and pulled up to pump #3. She turned the engine off and got out of the car, making sure to touch the rubber to ground herself, so she wouldn't be charged with static electricity. She walked around to the trunk of the car, got out the blue kerosene container, and close the trunk lid.

She slid the Credo's store debit card into to the machine and pre-paid for her gas. She pushed the 87 for regular unleaded fuel, and started to fill up the container with gasoline.

"Hey, honey, you know that is for kerosene, not gas, right?" a passerby pointed out.

"Yes, we all got to do what we go to do. My normal gas can broke leaving me with only this to use." Lynn smiled, watching him walk away. *Asshole*, she thought, as the container continued filling.

After she finished, she placed the container back in the trunk of the car and secured it. Last thing she needed was to be stopped for not having it secured correctly.

She closed the trunk lid and headed inside the convenience store, as she picked up her Samsung and called Michael.

"Heya, it's Lynn. Having fun?" she asked. "Are you with Raven still?"

"Yeah, she wanted to go see the rock concert last night that was in town. She wanted to see HIM play," Michael replied.

"Can you head home? Your dad needs to speak to you," Lynn continued. She had finished buying her drink from the shop and was on her way back to the car.

"Oh okay," he responded.

"I need to speak to Raven. Can you pass the phone over to her please?" Lynn questioned. A moment later, Raven's came over the phone.

"Hello, Lynn?" Raven began.

"Hey, Michael is going to take you back to his place. I need to speak to you out front. I got some bad news about your father," Lynn explained. She plugged the auxiliary cable back in, started the engine, and pulled out of the parking, while continuing the call over the car's audio system.

"What kind of news?" Raven inquired.

"It's best if I explain in person. I'm 20 minutes away. I'll meet you outside, okay? Just tell Michael not to stop for anything, he gets sidetracked a lot." Lynn ended the call, so she could concentrate on driving to Michael and Courtney's house.

~

"Good morning, Mrs. Hemlock. How are you today?" Lola remarked, welcoming her back to Credo's.

"Your student not here?" Mrs. Hemlock questioned.

"No, she isn't scheduled for today," Lola explained. "Your husband didn't join you today?"

"No, he is insisting he had to work. Said he had to deal with something. I don't know what," Sharon reported.

"Well, let me get you prepped and started, if you care to just sit here please." Lola offered a chair, spinning it around to let her sit down. Sharon took the seat offered and laid back as Lola draped an apron over her.

"I'm going to place the mask on your face again to protect your face from the water and shampoo, okay, Mrs. Hemlock?"

Sharon nodded, closing her eyes as the mask was placed over her face. Lola gathered up all the lose strands of hair and laid them in the sink as she filled it with water to let the hair soak.

"If you excuse me, I need to go to my office to retrieve my tools. I shall be back soon," Lola stated. She turned on the shop's radio, so she could listen to some music. "Just keep your hair in the water, Mrs. Hemlock, or we would have to do it again. The hair needs to get soaked, and I've placed a little oil into the water to treat your broken hair," Lola lied.

She walked over to her office sighing. She didn't know what Lynn was up to, but she trusted her. Seeing the note she'd left, Lola felt even more inclined to help Lynn, now more than ever. She walked around her desk and sat down to reread Lynn's note one more time.

~

Sarah looked at the dashboard clock in her car; it was almost five past ten. She reached over, picked up her siren, and placed it on top of her car, while starting to speed up. She knew where she had to go. She knew who would be in danger, and he would have no clue about it because she had his phone.

You don't have long left. You better call my cellphone before it's too late. Another text popped up on the phone just now.

She dropped the phone back onto the front passenger seat and floored it. She sped up to over 100mph, going as fast as she could through the streets of New York.

~

Lynn's red Dodge pulled up two houses down from Courtney's home. Looking in her rearview mirror, she saw Michael pulling up in front of the house. Lynn got out and waved to them. Michael waved back and headed inside the home, while Raven started to walk over to Lynn, who was still standing by her car.

Lynn walked to the back of the car and opened the trunk.

"Hi, Lynn, so what is the news?" Raven asked, as she walked up behind Lynn.

"Oh, hey, you mind giving me a hand with this? I'm just helping out. They're low on oil, and they didn't have hot water this morning," Lynn explained.

Raven reached into the trunk and helped lift the container.

"So, can I ask... do you love Chris?" Lynn wondered, as they started to walk toward the house. Lynn quickly used the iPhone to send another text.

You have two minutes. Last chance.

"Yes, I do. He was stuck on you for forever, even after you left," Raven tried to compliment her.

"I'm sorry to tell you, but your father is dead." Lynn suddenly announced. Raven froze in the street, staring at her.

"What? How?" she demanded.

"Well, on the level, Chris wanted to help you. He asked me for help, except he got carried away. He found out what your dad was doing to you. He cut his throat. I'll tell you the full story another time," Lynn explained, lightly tugging on her arm to get her moving again. "If you go around to the side, you will see the pipe that goes into. I'm going into make sure they have it primed to get going again."

Lynn stopped on the sidewalk and slipped the iPhone into Raven's pocket, as she watched Raven head around the side of the house before doubling back to her car.

Sarah picked up the phone again from the passenger seat. Seeing the latest text, she turned off the siren, as she was getting close and didn't want to tip her hand. She didn't really want to exactly help the cheating bum, but it was their fault he was in this position; although, it was on him that he cheated.

Sarah pressed on the *Call me* feature on the text, and it started to dial out as she put the phone to her ear.

Back in Credo's on the shelf above Mrs. Sharon, the phone started to vibrate. Lola heard the noise, but ignored it. The phone continued to vibrate as it slowly slipped off the shelf, bringing the burning hot curling iron with it. It fell directly on top of Sharon's head, scalding her before it landed in the water with the phone, electrocuting Sharon. She screamed loudly. Lola came bolting out from her office to see Sharon die, as it all happened so fast. At the same time, the fuse box for the entire building tripped, putting her and the shop into darkness.

When Lynn returned to the car, she turned around and leaned up against it. She watched Raven walk back to the front of the house and go inside.

Lynn used her Samsung phone to login to the home's wifi, and then logged into the app for their smart thermostat.

She loaded a pre-saved text with 6 pictures attached and hit send. Then, three things happened all at once.

Courtney's mom opened her phone and saw the pictures of her husband and Lynn. She immediately looked up at her husband, her eyes filled with pain and horror. All she saw next was his face engulfed in flame, as Lynn remotely triggered the iPhone in Raven's pocket to have the thermostat app start up the furnace. At the same time, Lynn heard the distinctive sound of a Desert Eagle being cocked behind her head.

As Lynn turned to face Sarah, the house exploded behind her.

"Thank you for taking care of Mrs. Howard for me," Lynn commented, with a smirk. "I told you, you were on the wrong side."

"What?" Sarah retorted, sounding confused. She'd been thrown off track as she was about to read Lynn her rights.

"You are going to want to get that," Lynn stated as Sarah's phone just started to ring.

Lynn stood there with a confident smile, as Sarah raised the phone to her ear. Blue was on the other end of the line, calling to inform her the Captain wanted everyone at Credo's. His wife had just been killed.

"I told you, sweetie."–Lynn started to walk past Sarah, ignoring the gun–"I'm a good person, and I would take care of your Captain's wife, except you did it for me. How you think it will go for you once they find out the last phone call was from you and you are the one who killed her?"–Lynn got in her car– "You coming?" Lynn asked, looking at Sarah through the open window.

The sounds of incoming sirens started to get louder as emergency services headed that way.

Sarah looked defeated. She lowered the gun and turned to stare at Lynn.

"How?" That was all Sarah could muster.

"Easy, I made you think I was trying to bluff him. Soon as I knew he was getting help, I knew I had to meet you and you showed me your style back in the club. As I learned, Sarah, people do not tend to display their weakness openly. If they do, it is normally so they can draw your attention away, which I did. And my final card on this hand, on the river, was Sharon, after I turned you. You just didn't know it," Lynn explained.

"So, the notifications and everything from England was not to lure Blue away, but to make me think you were trying to set him up?" The simplicity of the plan astounded Sarah as she began to realize how everything fit together.

"Well then, you coming with or you going to trust the legal system?"–Lynn brought her head back in the car and waited–"Who knows? You may get lucky. I mean, you didn't know you were a part of multiple felonies."

Sarah seemed to wake up from her daze as the sirens started to get even louder. She knew they would be there any minute. She ran to the other side of the car and got into the passenger seat.

Lynn lightly pressed the gas pedal and started to drive off at the modest 25mph speed limit. She turned off the street, and headed toward the main road.

She passed a fleet of firetrucks rushing by, as Lynn pulled over to the side of the road to let them pass.

"Nice hand," Sarah remarked, knowing she had been ahead of the game the whole time, until Lynn turned things around right at the end. She had just been rivered.